FRA

C000141162

THE ELL

Francis Vivian was born Arthur Ernest Ashley in 1906 at East Retford, Nottinghamshire. He was the younger brother of noted photographer Hallam Ashley. Vivian laboured for a decade as a painter and decorator before becoming an author of popular fiction in 1932. In 1940 he married schoolteacher Dorothy Wallwork, and the couple had a daughter.

After the Second World War he became assistant editor at the Nottinghamshire Free Press and circuit lecturer on many subjects, ranging from crime to bee-keeping (the latter forming a major theme in the Inspector Knollis mystery *The Singing Masons*). A founding member of the Nottingham Writers' Club, Vivian once awarded first prize in a writing competition to a young Alan Sillitoe, the future bestselling author.

The ten Inspector Knollis mysteries were published between 1941 and 1956. In the novels, ingenious plotting and fair play are paramount. A colleague recalled that 'the reader could always arrive at a correct solution from the given data. Inspector Knollis never picked up an undisclosed clue which, it was later revealed, held the solution to the mystery all along.'

Francis Vivian died on April 2, 1979 at the age of 73.

THE INSPECTOR KNOLLIS MYSTERIES
Available from Dean Street Press

The Death of Mr. Lomas

Sable Messenger

The Threefold Cord

The Ninth Enemy

The Laughing Dog

The Singing Masons

The Elusive Bowman

The Sleeping Island

The Ladies of Locksley

Darkling Death

FRANCIS VIVIAN

THE ELUSIVE BOWMAN

With an introduction by Curtis Evans

DEAN STREET PRESS

Published by Dean Street Press 2018

Copyright © 1951 Francis Vivian

Copyright © 2018 Curtis Evans

All Rights Reserved

Published by licence, issued under the UK Orphan Works
Licensing Scheme.

First published in 1951 by Hodder & Stoughton

Cover by DSP

ISBN 978 1 912574 39 1

www.deanstreetpress.co.uk

And thus I praye God that al fletchers getting theyr lyuynge truly, and al archers vsynge shootynge honestly, and al maner of men that fauour artillery, maye lyue continuallye in healthe and merinesse, obeying theyr prince as they shulde, and louing God as they ought, to whom for al thinges be al honour and glorye for euer.—Amen.

The Toxophilus of Roger Ascham, 1545 A.D.

INTRODUCTION

SHORTLY BEFORE his death in 1951, American agriculturalist and scholar Everett Franklin Phillips, then Professor Emeritus of Apiculture (beekeeping) at Cornell University, wrote British newspaperman Arthur Ernest Ashley (1906-1979), author of detective novels under the pseudonym Francis Vivian, requesting a copy of his beekeeping mystery *The Singing Masons*, the sixth Inspector Gordon Knollis investigation, which had been published the previous year in the United Kingdom. The eminent professor wanted the book for Cornell's Everett F. Phillips Beekeeping Collection, "one of the largest and most complete apiculture libraries in the world" (currently in the process of digitization at Cornell's The Hive and the Honeybee website). Sixteen years later Ernest Ashely, or Francis Vivian as I shall henceforward name him, to an American fan requesting an autograph ("Why anyone in the United States, where I am not known," he self-deprecatingly observed, "should want my autograph I cannot imagine, but I am flattered by your request and return your card, duly signed.") declared that fulfilling Professor Phillip's donation request was his "greatest satisfaction as a writer." With ghoulish relish he added, "I believe there was some objection by the Librarian, but the good doctor insisted, and so in it went! It was probably destroyed after Dr. Phillips died. Stung to death."

After investigation I have found no indication that the August 1951 death of Professor Phillips, who was 73 years old at the time, was due to anything other than natural causes. One assumes that what would have been the painfully ironic demise of the American nation's most distinguished apiculturist from bee stings would have merited some mention in his death notices. Yet Francis Vivian's fabulistic claim otherwise provides us with a glimpse of that mordant sense of humor and storytelling relish which glint throughout the eighteen mystery novels Vivian published between 1937 and 1959.

Ten of these mysteries were tales of the ingenious sleuthing exploits of series detective Inspector Gordon Knollis, head of the Burnham C.I.D. in the first novel in the series and a Scotland Yard detective in the rest. (Knollis returns to Burnham in later novels.) The debut Inspector Knollis mystery, *The Death of Mr. Lomas*, which was published in 1941, is actually the seventh Francis Vivian detective novel. However, after the Second World War, when the author belatedly returned to his vocation of mystery writing, all of the remaining detective novels he published, with two exceptions, chronicle the criminal cases of the keen and clever Knollis. These other Inspector Knollis tales are: *Sable Messenger* (1947), *The Threefold Cord* (1947), *The Ninth Enemy* (1948), *The Laughing Dog* (1949), *The Singing Masons* (1950), *The Elusive Bowman* (1951), *The Sleeping Island* (1951), *The Ladies of Locksley* (1953) and *Darkling Death* (1956). (Inspector Knollis also is passingly mentioned in Francis Vivian's final mystery, published in 1959, *Dead Opposite the Church*.) By the late Forties and early Fifties, when Hodder & Stoughton, one of England's most important purveyors of crime and mystery fiction, was publishing the Francis Vivian novels, the Inspector Knollis mysteries had achieved wide popularity in the UK, where "according to the booksellers and librarians," the author's newspaper colleague John Hall later recalled in the *Guardian* (possibly with some exaggeration), "Francis Vivian was neck and neck with Ngaio Marsh in second place after Agatha Christie." (Hardcover sales and penny library rentals must be meant here, as with one exception--a paperback original--Francis Vivian, in great contrast with Crime Queens Marsh and Christie, both mainstays of Penguin Books in the UK, was never published in softcover.)

John Hall asserted that in Francis Vivian's native coal and iron county of Nottinghamshire, where Vivian from the 1940s through the 1960s was an assistant editor and "colour man" (writer of local color stories) on the Nottingham, or Notts, *Free Press*, the detective novelist "through a large stretch of the coalfield is reckoned the best local author after Byron and D. H. Lawrence." Hall added that "People who wouldn't know Alan

Sillitoe from George Eliot will stop Ernest in the street and tell him they solved his last detective story." Somewhat ironically, given this assertion, Vivian in his capacity as a founding member of the Nottingham Writers Club awarded first prize in a 1950 Nottingham writing competition to no other than 22-year-old local aspirant Alan Sillitoe, future "angry young man" author of *Saturday Night and Sunday Morning* (1958) and *The Loneliness of the Long Distance Runner* (1959). In his 1995 autobiography Sillitoe recollected that Vivian, "a crime novelist who earned his living by writing . . . gave [my story] first prize, telling me it was so well written and original that nothing further need be done, and that I should try to get it published." This was "The General's Dilemma," which Sillitoe later expanded into his second novel, *The General* (1960).

While never himself an angry young man (he was, rather, a "ragged-trousered" philosopher), Francis Vivian came from fairly humble origins in life and well knew how to wield both the hammer and the pen. Born on March 23, 1906, Vivian was one of two children of Arthur Ernest Ashley, Sr., a photographer and picture framer in East Retford, Nottinghamshire, and Elizabeth Hallam. His elder brother, Hallam Ashley (1900-1987), moved to Norwich and became a freelance photographer. Today he is known for his photographs, taken from the 1940s through the 1960s, chronicling rural labor in East Anglia (many of which were collected in the 2010 book *Traditional Crafts and Industries in East Anglia: The Photographs of Hallam Ashley*). For his part, Francis Vivian started working at age 15 as a gas meter emptier, then labored for 11 years as a housepainter and decorator before successfully establishing himself in 1932 as a writer of short fiction for newspapers and general magazines. In 1937, he published his first detective novel, *Death at the Salutation*. Three years later, he wed schoolteacher Dorothy Wallwork, with whom he had one daughter.

After the Second World War Francis Vivian's work with the Notts *Free Press* consumed much of his time, yet he was still able for the next half-dozen years to publish annually a detective novel (or two), as well as to give popular lectures on a plethora of intriguing subjects, including, naturally enough, crime, but also fiction writing (he published two guidebooks on that subject), psychic forces (he believed himself to be psychic), black magic, Greek civilization, drama, psychology and beekeeping. The latter occupation he himself took up as a hobby, following in the path of Sherlock Holmes. Vivian's fascination with such esoterica invariably found its way into his detective novels, much to the delight of his loyal readership.

As a detective novelist, John Hall recalled, Francis Vivian "took great pride in the fact that the reader could always arrive at a correct solution from the given data. His Inspector never picked up an undisclosed clue which, it was later revealed, held the solution to the mystery all along." Vivian died on April 2, 1979, at the respectable if not quite venerable age of 73, just like Professor Everett Franklin Phillips. To my knowledge the late mystery writer had not been stung to death by bees.

Curtis Evans

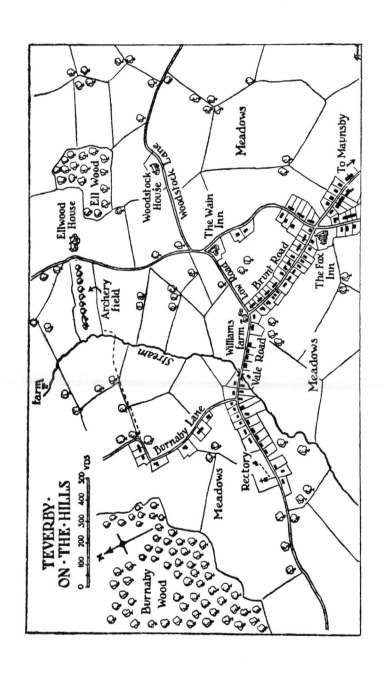

TEVERBY·
ON·THE·HILLS

0 100 200 300 400 500 yds

Burnaby Wood

Meadows

Rectory

Burnaby Lane

Meadows

Vale Road

Williams farm

Low Road

Stream

Archery field

farm

Ellwood House

Ell Wood

Woodstock House

Woodstock Lane

The Wain Inn

Brunt Road

The Fox Inn

Meadows

Meadows

To Maunsby

Chapter I
THE FOX AT TEVERBY

To obtain and keep the tenancy of an inn a man must have the untarnished character of an archbishop, the tact of a diplomat of the old school, and the business mind of a chartered accountant. On all counts Michael Maddison was eligible as the landlord of the Fox Inn at Teverby-on-the-Hills, the tenancy of which he acquired two years before Gordon Knollis came down from London to investigate the murder.

Maddison was a robust, healthy man of thirty-five, a dull-faced fellow with short-cropped brown hair, thickish lips, and a set of white teeth that were prominent whenever he smiled— and Maddison smiled a great deal. He was the genial if not jovial host, wandering round the house during opening sessions to have a word with each of his patrons. He could play darts and dominoes tolerably well, but not too well for the minority element which challenged him from time to time with the expressed object of winning free drinks. In the smoke-room he could talk intelligibly on a variety of subjects, but here again he knew when it was wise to withdraw, leaving the customer happy and self-satisfied in his own righteousness.

Rhoda, his sister, was two years his junior. Also unmarried, she fulfilled the duties of landlady and housekeeper. She was five feet six in height, two inches less than her brother, a good-looking and pleasant woman with high cheekbones, a smooth brow, a long aquiline nose, and a pleasant if somewhat thin mouth. She was slim and dark-complexioned, wearing her straight hair brushed back over her oval head and screwed into a tight bun at the nape of her neck; her small ears were set flat to her head, and from them hung emerald pendants, the only items of jewellery she ever wore.

She was of a quiet and reserved nature, moving about the inn with her hands clasped before her, smiling on all, but seldom speaking to them. She lived a private life within herself, and it was seldom she allowed even her brother to see into it. If he suggested that such-and-such would be a good idea, she said "Yes, Michael," and that was the end of it.

Living with the Maddisons was Gillian, their niece, a fresh and lively girl of twenty, the sole surviving member of their brother's family, which had otherwise been wiped out in one of the last London raids of the war. Gillian was working as secretary-typist to the manager of a firm of wine-merchants in Maunsby, the market town five miles from Teverby.

She had taken her Scottish mother's colouring, her auburn hair, blue eyes, cream complexion, and slim figure. Both sides of the family were strong-willed, and Gillian had inherited all the obstinacy and pertinacity they could hand on to her, so that at times Michael Maddison found himself engaged in a battle of wills from which he did not always emerge victorious, especially as Gillian had contrived to get herself engaged three times since coming to Teverby, and finally enraged Maddison by making a dead set at Captain Saunders of Ellwood House, who was twenty-two years her senior.

These three comprised the Maddison ménage, being assisted by Roberts, the cellarman, and two young village women who acted variously as daily helps, waitresses and barmaids.

Until Maddison's arrival the Fox had been just another village pub, capable of supplying beer and bread-and-cheese snacks. Maddison came with different if not entirely original ideas, and decided that an inn standing prominently on a crossroads linking two towns and a village was capable of catering for far more than the thirsts of the villagers and the occasional hunger of commercial travellers. Alterations were made at his suggestion and the brewery company's expense, and the Fox took a new lease of life.

"Pubs aren't drinking dens these days," said Maddison, flashing his white teeth at the company's agent, "but centres of communal life and homes-from-home for travellers, whether commercials or tourists. That's what they were intended to be, and actually were until the rise of the gin-palaces in the last century. I want to cater for the temperate man who likes to take his wife and kids out with him. I don't want him to have to leave them stewing in his car while he lobs in for a drink he has to rush down and can't enjoy."

"You have something," said the agent.

"I want a rose-garden behind the house," went on Maddison, "and a car-park to serve it. I want a few arbours sticking round it so that young couples can enjoy the illusion of privacy if not privacy itself. I want to draw a better class of custom to the house as well—the county set, for instance. They all spend money. Oh yes, and I want to cater for the social life of the village!"

He continued to smile winningly at the agent, putting all his undoubted charm into it. "I can't hope to cater for Captain Saunders' mania for archery, but he shoots on his own land, so that won't affect us at all. He is, however, forming a club in the village, and with a decent club-room instead of the barn-like place I've got I can persuade him to make his headquarters here. It will be a democratic and all-classes affair. Saunders says that in the days of Crecy and Agincourt every man from king to yeomen could handle a bow, and should still be able to do so . . ."

The agent sniggered. "Grown men playing at cowboys and Indians, eh?"

Maddison shook his head. "No! It isn't a sissy sport by any manner of means. Saunders had me down at his place last week, and after half an hour I found muscles I didn't know I owned. A four-feet wide target looks big at forty yards, but is devilish difficult to hit. Archery's a sport calling for strength, skill, and intelligence. That's beside the point, of course. With a decent clubroom I can get the archers here, and they'll give the lead to other clubs in the village which have, at present, to rent a dingy schoolroom for their meetings at ten bob a night. They'll get the use of my room for nothing, and I'll get the custom."

The agent nodded. "I think my directors will back your ideas, Mr. Maddison. They like initiative, and this place hasn't really paid its way for years. Get me rough plans of what you want, and I'll put them before the Board next week."

So the Fox was modernised. By the time Maddison, the architect, and the builders had done with it the inn was virtually a new house, with a dining-room looking out through French windows to a large bordered and arboured lawn which could serve as a tea-garden or beer-garden according to the time of day.

The club-room was contrived over the front porch, with a private staircase leading to a serving hatch at the end of the long bar, and also to a side door so that abstainers attending meetings could enter and leave without being subjected to the stares of regular patrons.

Captain Saunders' club came into existence as the Teverby Bowmen. It started with too much enthusiasm and forty-five members, six months after Maddison's arrival. In eighteen months it had sobered down, found its own level, and boasted twenty-six regular shooting members, six of whom were ladies, and included Rhoda and Gillian. Saunders was a good tutor, and by the end of the first season the club was able to put a sound team into the County Archery League.

The archery field was opposite Saunders' house, on Ellwood Road, half a mile from the Fox. Walking out of the Fox you crossed the main street and went down Uppercroft Lane, an S-bend, and up the hill past the Wain. As you descended the farther side of the hill you saw Ellwood House standing high on a bank on the right of the road, shielded from the east winds by the L-shaped wood from which it took its name.

At the foot of the hill, and on the left, was the archery field, lying flat in a narrow valley. It was two hundred yards long, and seventy wide, being divided down its length by a row of tall hawthorns. Halfway down the unobscured half of the field stood the target house, a sectional wooden shed eight feet by six feet and six feet high. Here were kept the targets, the easel-like target-stands, the arrow rests, and the measuring tapes for marking out the ground.

The remainder of the club equipment—the bows, arrows, and quiver-belts—was kept at Saunders' house, in a disused garden-room in the west which had an outside door leading from it, and a private path to a side gate opening to the road.

Most of the members had their own equipment by the end of the first eighteen months, but Saunders had insisted from the first, as chairman, that the club should buy four bows of different lengths and draw-weights, and not less than six dozen arrows.

"We may invite someone to try the game," he said at the inaugural meeting, "and if they don't fancy it they can go away without having wasted a shilling. If they join us they'll soon want their own tackle. The club tackle will help them while they're finding their feet, and will also serve as a useful stand-by in case of private breakages."

There was no objection to the suggestion. Captain Saunders knew his game. He had been a member of the Royal Toxophilite Society, and was not capable of leading them into any uneconomic policy.

He was a lean man of forty-two at the time of Maddison's tragic death, and possessed of a permanent tan acquired during many years of military service in the Middle and Far East. His manner of speech was clipped, and this, with his general air of briskness, tended to give strangers the impression that he was curt and uncivil. He wore a military moustache, an Engineer's tie, and plus-four tweed suits whenever his engagements required nothing more formal.

He was a favourite with the villagers, and a good mixer, although he tended to be unsocial when his nearest neighbour, Major Oliver of Woodstock House, steered the conversation to eastern philosophies, which he claimed to have studied at first hand, having, like Saunders, spent a good many years overseas.

Saunders said it must have been a different East to the one he knew. "Dunno where the deuce you found all your yogis, and gurus, and pandits, and pundits, and fakirs," he said. "I never found anything in the bazaars but bowl-bearing beggars, and fellows trying to twist the stupid Englishman of his hard-earned rupees."

"Seek, and ye shall find," Major Oliver replied sententiously. "When the pupil is ready the guru appears. Your remarks are in dam' bad taste!"

He was a bulky man with a stodgy body.

"Trouble with you, Saunders," he boomed, "is that you're an out and out materialist. Not blessed with any insight, you know! Still, that's your karma, and I mustn't judge you harshly, but I do think you should consider other people's feelings now and again."

Saunders shrugged. "Didn't intend to be offensive," he muttered. "We must help each other. You initiate me into this philosophical stuff, and I'll show you how to use a bow!"

"There you go again!" snorted the major. "A dirty dig at my somewhat full figure. Insinuating that I need exercise, eh? As for your bows and arrows—bah! You've never seen bows and arrows. Up in Mongolia I've seen bows of a hundred pounds strength—"

"Draw-weight," Saunders corrected him.

"Jargon," barked Major Oliver. "These things I'm talking about could kill a yak at forty yards!"

"So can a modern bow," Saunders said gently. "Perhaps I should say a bow used in the western world. I've hunting arrows at home that will go through one-eighth armour-plate at sixty yards."

"They sound interesting," said Maddison, who had been listening from the half-door over which he served. "I should like to see them!"

"So should I!" snorted Major Oliver.

"I'll bring a couple of samples along tomorrow night," said Saunders. "A broad-head, and a bodkin-pointed one. If you aren't satisfied when you've examined them we'll take them down to the field, and I'll show you how to put them through an old pitch-pine door at sixty yards."

Major Oliver's snortings degenerated into a low mumbling. "These bows were made of horn, backed with tendons," he said, determined not to lose the whole of the argument.

"The bow I'll use is made of yew, backed with degame."

"De—what?"

"Degame—popular name is lemonwood on account of its colour. Made by one of the best bowyers in the country—Cowan at Brookdale."

Major Oliver said: "Hm!"

Saunders smiled. "Drink up, Major, and let's have a loving-cup. Please, Mr. Maddison!"

Maddison pushed open the half-door and came to serve them. As he laid Saunders' change on the table a minute or so later, he said: "Think I could have a word with you before you go?"

Saunders lowered an eyebrow, and then lifted it high. "You mean you'd like to speak to me now?"

"That would be admirable," said Maddison.

Saunders excused himself to Major Oliver, and followed Maddison to the private sitting-room.

"I think you should know there's gossip in the village about Gillian and yourself," Maddison said in an apologetic voice as he closed the door.

Saunders gave a short and uncertain laugh. "Good lord! Is there? Who's saying what? In fact, who can say what?"

Maddison shrugged. "Usual village line, of course. Bluntly they're accusing you of making up to Gillian on the archery field. They say it's obvious, and think a man of your age shouldn't go kidnapping."

Saunders placed his hands on his hips, screwed up his mouth, and said: "Hm!"

He looked up at Maddison. "Any comments yourself?"

Maddison grimaced. "I'd like to hear from your own mouth whether there's truth in it or not. I'm her guardian for nearly another year."

"I've paid no more attention to Gillian than anyone else on the field," said Saunders. "I've had to teach them all, but none of them have had an unfair share of my time and attention. As a matter of fact, Gillian has probably had less of my time than the others. She's a natural, and such people have a genius for doing the right thing. She stands well, draws well without losing her energy—in fact she's a darned nice archer, Maddison! No, the gossip isn't fair. And I must remind you that I've twice taken your own sister to the theatre in town!"

"I had that in mind," said Maddison. "Point is that Gillian is at an impressionable and emotional age—on the verge of womanhood and all that. I'm satisfied she has a crush on you, and as man to man I'd like to ask you to discourage her. Keep her at arm's length, please."

"The whole thing is a shaker," said Saunders.

"That, and old Oliver chasing Rhoda," grimaced Maddison.

Saunders' eyebrow went up again. "Oliver—chasing Rhoda? Why, the old hound's fifty-seven if he's a day!"

"Which makes him as much older than Rhoda than you're older than Gillian—if you'll pardon my grammar," Maddison smiled grimly. "That's a point, actually. You'll appreciate how I feel about Gillian—or should have felt if there'd been any truth in the rumour. Anyway, come and have a drink with me. Sorry about this, but I had to mention it to you."

"Glad you did," murmured Saunders.

As they were going to the door Maddison said: "I'm not really keen on Rhoda marrying, either."

Saunders clicked his tongue. "Getting a bit heavy-handed, ain't you, old man? You mean you don't want either Rhoda or Gillian to get married at all?"

"That's the idea," said Maddison.

"By why the objection?" demanded Saunders.

"It would interfere with my plans."

Maddison leaned against the door, his right leg crossing his left, and his arms folded across his broad chest. The perfect white teeth were prominent in an ironical smile.

"Know what it is to want something so badly that you don't care what sacrifices you make providing you get it?"

"Can't say I do," replied Saunders. "Perhaps I've been lucky, but most of the things I've wanted have come drifting past, and I've only had to grab them."

"You've been lucky," said Maddison. "I've had to fight for everything I've ever wanted—barring my education. And I happen to want something very badly indeed."

"And this—er—want of yours entails a plan which in turn demands that neither of the girls shall marry?"

"That's it," said Maddison.

"Suppose one of them gets past you? Suppose you wake up one day and find that either Rhoda or Gillian has slipped past you, and is married?"

"That will be the day," Maddison said slowly.

"The day? What day?"

Maddison smiled, showing all his perfect white teeth. "The day I commit murder, Captain Saunders!"

He turned to open the door, and stood aside so that Captain Saunders could precede him. Two silent minutes elapsed, and then Gillian pushed open the second of the three doors leading into the room, and emerged from the side passage. She stood looking at the one through which Maddison and Saunders had passed, wiped a moist hand across her forehead, and hurried through to the kitchen.

Chapter II
THREE MOTIVES FOR MURDER

Michael Maddison's main fault was a complete inability to understand that other people had thoughts and feelings. It had, for instance, never occurred to him that his sister might have plans for her own life which excluded himself and his welfare. To him, never probing very deeply beneath the surface of affairs that did not benefit his own ego, it seemed she was perfectly content to devote the whole of her life to serving himself and his needs, and he would have been shocked if he had been able to look into her mind for a brief twenty seconds as she went mute and smiling about the inn with her hands elapsed lightly before her.

Rhoda, at thirty-three, was in revolt. Her life had been one of subjection, first to selfish parents who took her when her academic education was complete and turned her into a household slave, and then to Michael. She was secretly relieved when her father and mother contrived to die within a few months of each other. She saw the gates of freedom opening for her. Then Michael came back from his wanderings, and grabbed the symbolical collar round her neck before she had time to rid herself of it. He needed her. That was all he said. Rhoda was so conditioned to such stimuli that her reaction was automatic and unreflecting; she took over his housekeeping.

For a full year they lived in a cottage in a quiet Surrey lane, and then Michael took a holiday in the East Midlands and came home to announce that he had taken the tenancy of a village inn. Rhoda blinked once, and said: "Oh!"

Later, in the privacy of her room, she sat on the edge of her bed and began to think for perhaps the first time in her life. Her thoughts were long ones, reaching far into the future. She made plans, and Michael was not included in them. They were mainly concerned with the business of getting herself married and being the mistress, instead of the servant, in a house of her own. No longer would she be dominated. Blood was thicker than water, but distasteful to the palate. She would go with Michael to the Midlands, outwardly obedient as ever, and then one day she would walk out of the house and into a church, emerging on the arm of a man she would call her husband.

Two years went by at the Fox at Teverby, two years during which she looked for a suitable man, and two years during which she tried to penetrate Michael's mind and learn why he had twice buried them, once in a Surrey lane, and again in a village like *this*.

On the night when Michael had talked with Captain Saunders she had been serving in the long saloon, and had seen them go to the sitting-room. Handing the bar over to Rose Cromwell, the elder of the barmaids, she went upstairs, ostensibly to fetch a handkerchief. Having banged her door noisily, she went down the back stairs to the kitchen, carrying her shoes in her hand, and from there listened to the conversation through the communicating door. She was back in the saloon with no more than a few seconds to spare when the two men reappeared in the bar. Outwardly she was as bland as ever, but her brain was working swiftly behind the sleek *façade*.

Neither she nor Gillian were to be allowed to marry. Gillian was young, and the ban was possibly allowable in her case, but to be treated as a child when one was thirty-three was a different matter. The reason for Michael's attitude did not interest her in the least. The probable effect of his ban interested her a great deal. She was satisfied that Harry Saunders wanted to marry her, even if he had not yet proposed, and that was all she needed to know. Old Oliver was still there if needed, but it was Harry she wanted, and intended to get!

How did Michael hope to enforce his ban? That was the mystery. How could he prevent her from marrying? Was he relying on will-power alone, on her conditioned subservience to his wishes. If so, then Michael was in for the shock of his life! She would force the pace with Harry, and within three months be his wife, leaving Michael to scratch his head and do just what the— yes, just what the hell he liked about it! She was roused to the point where she could even swear, skimming away the veneer of social manners taken unto herself in the convent school in which her education began.

After closing-time that night, and when the staff had gone home, she went to Michael in the bar while he was cashing up.

"Michael," she said firmly, "I had a surprise tonight. I accidentally overheard some of your conversation with Harry Saunders."

Michael barely looked up from the cash scattered on the counter. "Did you?" he murmured. "So what?"

"I'm not interested in your reasons, but I am interested in your intention to stop me marrying him."

"Nine-ten, ten pounds, ten-ten, ten-fifteen, and two pounds in coppers makes twelve-fifteen, including the floater. A poor day!" said Michael. "There's twelve-eighteen on the roll, which means somebody's either been slack or on the fiddle."

"And why are we buried in this damned awful village?" Michael tapped his fingers on the counter, and re-checked the till-roll.

"I asked you a question, Michael!"

"I don't answer questions," said Maddison.

"If Harry asks me to marry him, I shall do so."

"If Saunders even asks you to marry him he'll wish he hadn't," said Michael. He shovelled the cash into a canvas bag and tied the neck of it. "Rose was on the till for the last hour, so I'll stop the three shillings from her wages. I'm not running this place merely for the fun of it!"

"I'd remind you, Michael, that I am of an age generally described as *of discretion*," Rhoda said primly.

"Then exercise it," said Michael.

"I shall marry him!"

"You'll marry when I say you can," Michael replied. "Do as you're told, woman!"

Rhoda gave a short and sardonic laugh and turned to walk from the bar. "I fancy your egotistical and thick-headed ideas are going to be badly shaken in the near future, Michael!"

The canvas bag rattled on the counter. Michael reached a long arm toward her, grasped her by the shoulder, and pulled her back.

"If you marry Saunders I'll murder you both!"

"You talk like a third-rate thriller!" Rhoda snapped.

Michael's hand struck her full across the mouth.

"Go to bed!"

Rhoda ignored the thin stream of blood trickling down her chin. For one long second she stared steadily at him, and then walked to the foot of the stairs, mounting them with dignity. She smiled as she reached the head of the stairs. Gillian's bedroom was closing silently. So much the better if she had heard the quarrel! She might be moulded into a valuable witness, if not more, in the course of time. Her mind was made up. If she was ever to live her own life, and enjoy freedom, there was one thing she must do—she must murder her brother Michael!

In her own room, Gillian Maddison walked to the dressing-table, fluffing the auburn hair from her slim shoulders. The eavesdropping was justifiable since it had clarified her own position in the house. Michael—she never called him Uncle—was, for some reason or other, prepared to murder anyone who wanted to marry either Rhoda or herself, and Rhoda, the bitch, was prepared to get Harry by hook or by crook. She poised a finger on her lip as she regarded herself in the mirror. It was going to be difficult. Even with Rhoda out of the way she would still have Michael to contend with, so *that* was out! She couldn't be happy without Harry, so it looked as if—as if it would have to be Michael!

She wanted Harry because she loved him, and not as Rhoda wanted him, just to say she was a married woman and be clear of the spinster's shelf. Both Michael and Rhoda thought she was immature, still stumbling through the awkward stages of puberty, and in love with love rather than with Harry. She clenched her jaw with all the obstinacy of her Scottish ancestors. She'd get Harry, and Rhoda, the old fool, could put up with that other old fool, Oliver, who was chasing her like a sensation-seeking boy of seventeen.

She banished the frown from her pretty face, and smiled winningly at herself. She slipped from her clothes, letting them lie unheeded at her feet as she slid smooth hands down her svelte and virginal figure. She laughed. Rhoda hadn't a chance against her, the stuffy and shapeless creature!

The thing to do now was widen the breach between Michael and Rhoda. She knew she had always been Michael's weakness, and could do more with him than anyone else on earth. She'd have a confidential talk with him, asking for his worldly advice, appealing in her apparent innocence to his vast—so vast!—experience of the world.

There was no time like the present. She put on her eau-de-nil pyjamas, threw a peach boudoir wrap over her shoulders, and plunged her feet into the waiting mules. She carefully disarranged her auburn hair, and went forth into battle.

She knocked lightly on Michael's door. He opened it after a few seconds, tying the cord of his dressing gown, and said: "Oh! Hello!"

"Can I come in, Michael dear," Gillian said softly. "It's the only time I can catch you when Aunt Rhoda isn't hanging round with both ears open."

He smiled fondly at her as he closed the door behind her and led her across the room to his bedside chair. "What's the trouble, Jill?"

She chose his bed, and curled upon the coverlet, her hands clenched between her knees. "I can't sleep, darling! I'm worried—ever so worried!"

He laughed at her. "Worried at your age? You shouldn't have a blessed care in the world!"

"Michael," she said in a tone of deep concern. "Have you ever been in love?"

"What man hasn't?" he said simply.

"I know," Gillian sighed, "but you seem above most men, as if you always had such great things in your mind that love seems trivial to you."

She sighed again, and hoped she wasn't laying it on too heavily. It was difficult to tell with Michael.

"I was in love once, Jill, madly and badly. That was a long time ago."

"You—you lost her?" Gillian asked in a carefully-contrived tone of intense sympathy.

"I lost her," said Michael. He shrugged. "So what? But who's damaging your little heart, because I'll wring his neck if you ask me."

"It isn't a *him* that's the trouble," Gillian said pointedly.

"You've a rival?"

"She's such greater advantages," said Gillian. "She's older, and more experienced, and uses *tricks*."

"Who's the man?" asked Michael, suddenly suspicious.

"Harry Saunders, and I love him! I do love him, Michael!"

Michael's mouth tightened. "Rhoda?"

Gillian stared at the coverlet and sighed dramatically. Michael's voice came to her like an unpleasant tune played on long-rusty strings. "Gillian, you'll forget all about marriage, and about Saunders. For one thing he's too old for you, and old and new wines cannot be mixed without turning both sour. For another thing I don't want you to marry, not just yet."

"You're siding with Aunt Rhoda!"

"I've also forbidden your aunt to marry!"

Gillian looked up with wide eyes and parted lips. "But she's old, Michael! She can do as she likes!"

"Let her try it," Michael said grimly.

He cocked an ear, and strode silently to the door, snatching it open. Rhoda was standing there, as if her right ear had been pressed to the woodwork. Michael's arm came back for the second time that night, and his fist took her clean on the side of the jaw, so that she rocked on her heels and collapsed in the middle of the corridor.

Gillian slid from the bed, pushed past Michael, and ran to her aunt. In a split second, and for a short period of time, Rhoda was no longer her rival, but another woman, a fellow-member of the Sisterhood of Eve, a fraternity capable of sinking private differences when faced by a common enemy. Rhoda smiled dazedly as Gillian helped her to her feet.

"Thank you, darling," she said. "I'll be all right. I'm getting accustomed to it. Our Michael, our knight without reproach, is beginning to show us what he really is—an oaf and a bully. I think he must have spent the last few years among savages." She walked unsteadily back to her room.

Gillian looked angrily at Michael. He was framed in the doorway, his hands resting on the lintel above his head, a mocking smile on his round face, and the white teeth prominent even in the half-light of the corridor.

"The comedy is over, Jill," he said pleasantly. "You can act almost as well as your aunt!"

Gillian narrowed her eyes. "If you interfere between Harry and myself—I'll kill you, Michael!"

Michael let his arms fall to his sides. "If you aren't in your room within thirty seconds I'll turn you over my knee and spank you for the silly and melodramatic child you are!" Gillian went.

At half-past nine the next morning Michael went into town for a discussion with the company's architect. He had another idea, wanting a dividing wall between two of the cellars taken out so that one long cellar would result. He explained it over breakfast, treating Rhoda and Gillian as if the events of the previous night had never happened. His view was that the removal of the wall would save a lot of unnecessary work for Roberts and the delivery men. "And I'm all for saving work if it can be arranged," he said.

As soon as he was clear of the house, and Gillian safely at business, Rhoda rang Harry Saunders and asked if he could spare ten minutes if she slipped along to see him. She told the two helps that she had to see Mrs. Langdon about the garden party being organised by the Women's Institute, and cycled down the village and back along Low Road to Ellwood House.

Saunders met her at the door, and at once wanted to know the cause of the bruise on her jaw.

"That's what I want advice about," she said grimly.

Saunders took her into the library and poured her a port. "Get that down. You look all in."

"I had very little sleep," she said.

"Michael did it, of course?" Saunders asked in a deliberately casual voice.

"Can we take the lid off and talk as man to man, with no punches pulled?" Rhoda asked, descending to the vernacular under the emotional strain.

"I think we understand each other," said Saunders.

"I overheard the talk you had with Michael—or Michael had with you."

"Oh!" said Saunders, and turned to look through the window at his lawns.

"I challenged Michael when the place was closed, and he smacked my mouth and told me I was under his orders—me, a woman, of twenty-nine," she said, conveniently confusing the two incidents and deducting the date from her age.

"What do you know about Michael's past life?" Saunders asked from the window.

"Practically nothing," Rhoda said slowly, "He went through Sandhurst—"

"An army man?" Saunders interrupted. "I'd no idea!"

"An army man," nodded Rhoda. "He had postings all over the world, and I never saw him for years at a time. He came back to England three years ago with the rank of lieutenant-colonel."

Saunders turned suddenly. "Lieutenant-colonel? Then why the deuce—"

"Bury us in Teverby? That's what I want to know," said Rhoda, walking to the window and standing beside him. "He first buried us in a quiet lane in Surrey, and then came here. I don't understand him, Harry, I never did."

"Why should he want to prevent you getting married?"

"Us," Rhoda said pointedly.

Saunders grunted. "Even to considering murder. He made it sound as simple and ordinary as the act of shaving every morning."

"Almost as if he was accustomed to murdering!"

"You may have something there," said Saunders.

Rhoda toyed nervously with the wine glass, twirling the stem between her fingers. "You—you do want me, Harry?"

He looked askance at her. "You should know the answer to that, Rhoda!"

She slid the glass on the window-sill. "I won't keep you waiting longer than necessary, Harry, but I'm in no mood for endearments and embraces at the moment."

"No, of course not," murmured Saunders.

"We have to find a way of fixing Michael first."

"If we could get at his private papers," said Saunders cryptically.

"They're in the desk in the room you were in last night. He carries the keys with him, in his hip pocket."

She glanced at the clock. "I must run. I'm supposed to be seeing Mrs. Langdon, and Michael is quite capable of ringing her when he gets back, so I'll have to call. You'll be in tonight?"

"As usual," said Saunders. He escorted her to the gates at the end of the drive, silent and thoughtful.

She smiled wistfully as she mounted her cycle. "We'll have all the time in the world when we've settled Michael!"

"All the time in the world," said Saunders.

He watched her cycle up the hill, and then hurried through to the summer-house where Gillian was waiting for him. "You've been so long, my darling," she whispered as she flung her arms round his neck. "It seemed ages!"

"Aunt Rhoda," he said grimly, "wanting advice on how to circumvent Michael and marry me!"

"Why don't you tell her the truth? Why don't you give her the bullet?" Gillian demanded urgently.

"Can't be done, sweetheart," said Saunders as he slid his arms round her waist. "If we antagonise Rhoda we'll find ourselves up against a formidable combination."

Gillian laid her cheek on his shoulder. "What *are* we going to do about him, Harry darling?"

"Do you love them a great deal?"

"I hate Rhoda, and I wouldn't trust Michael as far as I could see him with one eye."

"You see," Saunders said softly, "I'm getting desperate. I want you so badly. If Michael was to be found dead, and if it was proved that Rhoda had killed him because he stopped her from marrying me . . ."

"That's—that's murder!"

"Yes, it's murder, but even murder is justifiable at times. The penal law is one thing, and the moral law an entirely different one."

Gillian put her hand over his mouth. "Harry—please don't talk like that! We mustn't. I lay awake all last night thinking about murder, and then as the sun came up I saw that it was all wrong. We mustn't, Harry!"

He moved her hand from his mouth and kissed it. "Sorry darling. We're getting overwrought. I'll think of something, don't worry. Now what about getting you into town before some nosey villager sees you?"

She clung tightly to him. "You do love me, Harry?"

"I do love you, Gillian!"

"And you *are* going to marry me and make an honest woman of me?"

"You are an honest woman, darling, and I am going to marry you!"

"I worship you, Harry!"

"You shouldn't," said Saunders. "No man is worth it—"

"You are!"

"And worship should be reserved for our Maker," Saunders went on.

"I still worship you! I'd do anything, anything in the world for you—even to—to murder!"

"Listen, Gillian," said Saunders. "There's a thing to be mentioned. Don't let yourself slip and give the show away if Rhoda taunts you by saying I'm going to marry her. She's gone away with that idea. I daren't let her do any other. Those who aren't for us are against us. Better to let her think what she does than let her go over to Michael's side. There's something wrong somewhere—something nasty and dangerous, and I can't put my finger on it. We have to find out what it is. Michael's papers should help. I must get into your house one night when you're all asleep . . ."

"Second bedroom on the right of the landing," said Gillian.

"Sitting-room downstairs," said Saunders.

"But you do love me, Harry?"

"That's why I stay in the sitting-room!"

Hand in hand they went to the garage for the car. Saunders ran her along Woodstock Lane to the outskirts of Maunsby, from where she caught a bus into town.

Back at the Fox, Rhoda had immediately telephoned to Gillian's place of business. It was her intention to pretend to take Gillian into her confidence, and to pretend to help her with her courtship of Harry Saunders. That way she would know what was happening around her, and there was also a plan whereby she could foist the guilt for Michael's forthcoming death on Gillian's slim shoulders. So she was surprised when told that Gillian had not arrived at the office.

Rhoda stood with the receiver in her hand for a full minute after the call was closed, and then slapped it down and went to Michael's room for the field-glasses that were kept in the bottom of his wardrobe. If Gillian wasn't in the office, there was only one other place where she could be, and as she had to get to the office sometime during the morning there was only one way she could logically take without being seen in the village.

Rhoda hurried to the attic at the top of the house, drew up a rickety bentwood chair, and watched a section of Woodstock Lane which could be seen through a gap between two of the houses diagonally opposite the inn.

She was prepared to wait all day, or until Michael returned for lunch, but only a quarter of an hour elapsed before a long rakish sports car sped from the direction of Ellwood Road towards Maunsby. There were two people in it; a man in a sports jacket, and a girl whose auburn hair was streaming out in the wind. The girl's head was on the man's shoulder, and his left arm was around her.

She put the glasses in their case and returned them to Michael's wardrobe. That settled it! She had to make haste! None of them were to be trusted. Not even Harry.

CHAPTER III
THE VANISHING ARROWS

CAPTAIN SAUNDERS took his hunting arrows to the Fox the same evening, a bodkin-pointed one and a broadhead, both capable of piercing armour-steel from a respectable distance. Even Major Oliver was impressed, and nodded his head many times as he examined them.

"Very good, Saunders! Better than I expected. Never object to admitting when I'm wrong. Deadly weapons indeed. Yes, my old friends in Mongolia would gladly accept them as a present."

He handed them to Maddison, who gingerly tested the points on his thumb. Maddison grinned. "I wouldn't want one in my gizzard even from a hundred yards!"

"I'm still prepared to demonstrate if there are any doubting Thomases amongst us," smiled Saunders. He brushed his clipped moustache with a superior, almost insolent gesture. "How about taking part in a William Tell act, Maddison?"

Maddison grinned. "Not unless you're to be the one to balance the apple!"

"Offer not taken," said Saunders.

A motor coach drew up outside, and almost at once the inn began to fill with trippers on their way back from the coast. Maddison was moving to the bar when Saunders stayed him.

"Mind putting these under the counter or somewhere until I go home. They aren't things to have lying about, and if these people have had a previous pull-up they may be ripe for horseplay."

Maddison took the arrows behind the bar, and laid them on the wide shelf below the wine and spirit bottles. "You'll be able to keep an eye on them there, and reach them when you go," he called to Saunders. He appeared to be thinking deeply about something or other.

Rhoda came into the bar a minute or so later. Her eyes went straight to the arrows. Then a fat and demanding customer called an order, and she turned to help Michael. A few minutes later she pressed a bell-push under the till to call Gillian, who helped when business became heavy. She served the smoke-room, and from the moment she appeared Rhoda kept her and Saunders under observation.

Rhoda, in a slack moment, contrived to test the points of the arrows as her brother had done. Looking up into the mirrors that lined the wall behind the shelves, she saw Gillian watching her closely over the half-door leading from the smoke-room. She smiled a secret smile and helped herself to a pink gin.

For some reason not apparent to anyone in the house, Michael developed a temper. It began with a sulky expression, grew into glowering surliness, and eventually became a thin-lipped and silent hymn of hate. At last, muttering to himself, he pushed past Rhoda and went round the glass-panelled partition to the tap-room pumps, which were being operated by Roberts, the cellar-man.

"What the deuce have you done with the beer on numbers four and five?" he demanded. "It's coming up like soapsuds!"

Roberts, a tubby little man, looked at him, stuck a wondering tongue in his cheek, and went along the bar to the offending pumps. He put a glass under one of them and drew a sample.

"That's clear enough," he remarked. He emptied it into the draining tray, and tried a sample from the neighbour pump.

"What's the idea, Mr. Maddison?" he asked bluntly. "The stuff's as clear as isinglass, and there's no more froth than there should be. It's not like you to complain of my cellar-work!"

"That stuff's no good to me!" snapped Maddison. "I've strangers in tonight, and I want them to go away giving the house a good name."

"It won't get a bad one on this ale," Roberts retorted.

"Who's the landlord? Who has to sell it?" demanded Maddison.

Roberts clicked his tongue, and went through to the lobby. He pulled the strings of his apron, rolled it into an untidy ball, and threw it on the side-table. "I'll fetch my cap and coat, and see you in the morning, Mr. Maddison. You'll perhaps feel better then, and in a mood to apologise!"

"I'll do my own cellaring first!" snapped Maddison.

Roberts nodded. "That's okay with me, sir, I've another job waiting. I'll call for my cards on Friday—when you're out."

"I'll post them to you, together with what I owe you." Roberts went to the kitchen for his clothes, and as he came back he said: "You owe me nothing but an apology. If you do think you owe me anything, then make it a dose of salts, and take 'em yourself when you go to bed."

He pushed open the swing doors, letting them flap to and fro as he walked into the village street.

Maddison went back to the bar, seeming more pleased with himself. He found a good number of curious eyes on him, but refused to meet them, and went behind the partition to take over the tap-room trade.

It was half an hour later when Rhoda went to him. He was humming a tune to himself.

"Harry Saunders can't find his arrows, Michael."

"They're on the shelf behind the bar. He saw me put them there!"

"They were," said Rhoda, "but they aren't there now!"

Maddison put an order on a tray and pushed it through the hatch. "Think he's pulling your leg?"

"I hope nobody else pulls it with such a lack of humour," she replied tartly.

"His arrows just are not there!" Maddison sighed, and followed her to the hatch, where Saunders was waiting.

"My arrows, please, old man!" said Saunders.

"I haven't moved them," said Maddison. He looked round the saloon bar, put his hands to his mouth, and called Rose Cromwell across.

"Have you seen Captain Saunders' two arrows?"

"Saw you put them on the shelf," she said with northern brevity.

"I know I put them on the shelf," snapped Maddison, "but they aren't there now!"

"In that case they're gone," she said, and went back to take more chaff from a customer at the other side of the room.

"Gone!" echoed Maddison.

He turned to Saunders. "You were sitting straight opposite the hatch. Didn't you see anybody take them?"

"Don't ask silly questions!" Saunders retorted. "If I'd seen them go I wouldn't be asking for them. I was talking, not keeping my west eye on the bar. Why should they go? They're of no use to anyone but an archer. Anyway, a joke's a joke, so suppose you call it a day?"

The arrows were not to be found. Maddison and Saunders went from room to room, pleading with anyone who had taken them to return them to Captain Saunders, who wished to be going home. The arrows were not to be found.

Rose Cromwell saw them the next morning while dusting the lobby in her own inimitable manner, which was to dust anything that came a foot above or a foot below the eye-level, but nothing else.

Michael's golf-bag was hanging on the hook behind the right-hand swing door, and she decided to give the top of the shafts a birthday; they were looking a wee bit grey. She took the bag down, and flashes of colour attracted her eye—the flights of the two missing arrows, two green and one white feather on each arrow.

She turned them over in her hands, and then dropped them back into the bag and lifted it to its hook. The best thing to know in the Fox at Teverby was nothing, sweet nothing. That way you didn't get yourself into trouble.

She flicked her way into the smoke-room, pondering on the strangeness of the matter. Curiosity urged her to glance in the bag again on the following morning. The arrows were no longer there. Someone, she decided, had taken them.

The builders' men came four days later, and began to knock the cellars about. They tore down a section of the ceiling, made two large holes in the walls, and fitted a heavy steel beam, after which they took down the dividing wall, making what had been two cellars into one large one forty-seven feet long and twenty feet wide.

The builders were followed by a joiner, who built a large double-doored cupboard on the end wall opposite the delivery chute. It was shelfless, and fitted with a strong mortice lock, and two bolts on the inside of the left-hand door. Rhoda and Gillian, still outwardly friendly, could make no sense of the alteration, but knowing Michael as they now did, asked no questions. Michael did not answer questions.

From this time certain changes took place in the routine of the inn. Michael, who had previously risen at half-past eight each morning, now found it necessary to be out of bed at least an hour earlier in order, he said, to do Roberts' cellar-work. Surprising them both, he took cups of tea to bed ten minutes after rising, and seemed to be his old genial self once more.

Previously, too, he had tended to resent Rhoda's use of the car. Now, whenever she hinted at an alleged emptiness of the larder, he almost pushed her to the garage, and the car to the road, and when Gillian cautiously suggested spending her week's holiday at the sea with a girl-friend with whom she worked, Michael readily agreed, waving aside a mild objection by the spinsterish-minded Rhoda.

"She's no longer a child," he said sharply. "It's time she began to find her way about the world."

"I thought she already knew it," said Rhoda, and hurriedly left the room.

While Gillian was away, Rhoda forced the pace with Harry Saunders, deciding that her years should give her an advantage over Gillian, and hoping that, despite the attraction between them, she could push Gillian from the picture. She lost three days work on him when he found it necessary to go to London on business, but was comforted by receiving two letters from him on the notepaper of the hotel at which he was staying, both bearing West-One postmarks. They proved to her complete satisfaction that he had not slipped away to the coast to see Gillian. She was winning the good fight.

Saunders was due back on the same evening as Gillian, but rang through early in the evening to say his business had taken longer than expected, and he would take the eight o'clock down-train. This did not arrive in Maunsby until midnight, and so he would call to see her in the morning.

Despite her growing hatred of Gillian, Rhoda's maternal instinct still compelled her to keep a watchful as well as a wary eye on her, and she was disturbed when she had not arrived home by eleven o'clock. She was wondering what to do when the telephone bell rang for the second time that night. Gillian was on the line to say she had arrived in Maunsby, but would spend the night with Sally, going straight on to business in the morning, and returning home in the evening. Was this all right with Aunt Rhoda? Rhoda said it would be now she knew where she was.

A new feminine voice came on the line. "Sally Denby here, Miss Maddison! We've had a lovely time, and I'm glad you don't mind Jill staying with me. It will top the holiday nicely. Thanks ever so much!"

"That is quite all right, dear," said Rhoda. "Say goodnight to Gillian for me, please."

She was smiling as she turned away from the instrument. Gillian would now be out of the way until late tomorrow evening!

"Who was that?" asked Michael as he entered the room.

"Gillian. She's staying with her friend Sally tonight, Sally was also on the 'phone, so it will be all right."

Michael gave a short laugh. "If it's been all right for a week it should be for one more night—or vice versa. Gillian may be a strong-willed little devil, but she's moral!"

"Did I say she was anything else?" Rhoda asked with prim dignity.

"No, but you were thinking it—or hoping it," said Michael.

"Oh, men," snapped Rhoda, and went to bed.

Michael looked into her room at midnight. "Still awake?"

"I can't read when I'm asleep," said Rhoda. "Why?"

"You'd better slip something on and get down to the 'phone. Your tom-fool lover is wanting a word with you. He's in a call-box at the station at Maunsby, and short of coppers. Midnight! Tchk-tchk!"

"What are you doing at this time of the night?" Rhoda asked as she reached for her wrap. "You haven't been to bed?"

"Trying to get the accounts in order to save time at the end of the month."

"Of course!" Rhoda said happily, and hurried down to the telephone. Victory indeed, when Harry rang her at midnight! Where was little Gillian now, in spite of her pussy-cat smile and fluffy auburn hair! She could have kissed even Michael just now.

"Speaking from town," said Saunders, "while I'm waiting for my taxi to roll up. Everything all right?"

"Everything's lovely!" Rhoda enthused. "It's nice to hear your voice. You'll call tomorrow?"

"You know!" replied Saunders. "Well, here's the taxi. Look after yourself!"

Michael was leaning on the door-frame as she turned away, smiling at her over the littered table. "I could almost hate myself for holding up your affairs, Rhoda," he said, "but there are good reasons. Just be patient, and trust me."

"I don't really mind waiting, Michael," she said softly as she came up to him. "I know I can trust you. Goodnight, dear."

Knowing Michael would be downstairs for some time, she went past her bedroom door and up the second flight of stairs to the attic. There she waited in the filmy darkness of the June night, and watched. Two long fingers of light eventually appeared on Woodstock Lane from the direction of town, and sped toward Ellwood House. She watched them vanish behind the houses, and went happily to bed.

At nine o'clock the next morning Rose Cromwell walked to the back door of the inn, turned the knob, and banged her nose as she tried to walk through a locked door. That was unusual. She knocked, and then realised that the bedrooms were at the front of the house, and if either Mr. or Miss Maddison were upstairs, or in the smoke-room or the saloon, they would not hear her. She went round the side-door, the one that led variously to the club-room, the lobby, and the serving hatch. She knew the latch should be fastened back, so she pushed the door and it swung open, but with a peculiar little click she had not noticed before.

All was strangely quiet inside. She looked in the bar, and then padded into the kitchen. The fire was not lit, there was no breakfast on the table, and the sink held only last night's supper dishes. It was blooming queer!

She looked at the bank of switches as she came back to the bar. They were all at Off, which meant there was no one in the cellar. She walked to the open side door, scratching her head. Robinson, the local constable, was standing on the opposite corner, either waiting for his sergeant or his time to go off duty. She called him across.

"What's wrong, Rose?" he asked. He was a tall thin man who looked as if he thought life was just a huge joke.

"Don't know," she said shortly. "Back door was locked when I came in, but this one was off the latch. Nobody's had any breakfast, and there doesn't seem to be anybody in the place."

"Perhaps taking an extra hour in bed," Robinson suggested.

"Ye-es, they might be at that!" Rose admitted. "I'll run up to her room—but you wait here!"

Rhoda was sitting up in bed, rubbing her eyes when Rose put her head round the door.

"Morning, Miss Maddison! You haven't half slept! It's turned nine by a good piece. Fair startled me when I couldn't find anybody about."

Rhoda blinked heavily. "Turned nine? Nobody about? Then where's Mr. Michael?"

"Don't know, ma'am. Can't see any signs of life downstairs. There's no fire, and he's had no breakfast."

"How odd!" commented Rhoda. "He must be in bed—but if he is, how did you get in?"

"Side door was off the latch, ma'am. I'll see if he's in bed."

Michael was not in bed, although his bed had been slept in. Rose went back to report.

"But he must be somewhere downstairs," said Rhoda. "Is he in the cellar?"

"The stairs light is off, ma'am."

"Surely I can hear him coughing?" said Rhoda.

"That's Robinson, ma'am. I didn't like the look of things, and fetched him in."

Rhoda laughed. "Silly girl! Go downstairs, and I'll get up. He's bound to be somewhere around the place."

Rose went back to Robinson. "There's something funny. She's in bed, but he isn't."

"You say this side door was undone?"

"How else did I get in—down the chimney?"

"He's probably having a natter in the village," said Robinson. "He isn't like you and me, having to get to work on time. He's his own boss."

"There's something wrong," Rose persisted. "I can smell it!"

"That's the beer," grinned Robinson. He looked at the wall clock. "You've four minutes in which to find me a nice body, and then I'm going home! Should have been off duty hours ago only

I was trying to catch Wilson coming in with a load of out-of-season game—and then I missed him."

Rose went to the switchboard, and flicked on the light at the head of the cellar steps. "I won't rest until I've looked round. One or two queer things have been happening . . ."

Her voice became indistinct as she vanished down the stone steps. Then she screamed, and screamed again. Robinson ran down to her, asking what had got into the hysterical woman. He came to a shocked halt in the middle of the cellar floor. Both lights were on, and Rose was standing against the switches. The farther lamp had a string tied through a hole in its shade, and the other end of the string was drawn up to a nail in the ceiling, so that the light was focussed on the double-doored cupboard.

At the foot of the cupboard lay Michael Maddison, a green and white fletched arrow sticking from his ribs. A second arrow, similarly fletched, was buried deeply in the right door of the cupboard.

"Is he—is he . . . ?" Rose asked tremulously.

Robinson bent over him. "He's dead all right. Taken him clean through the heart. It's murder, Rose. That's what it is—murder!"

Chapter IV
THE INITIAL INQUIRY

ROBINSON'S SERGEANT was waiting for him at the opposite side of the street, and was urgently beckoned across to the inn. He entered the lobby as Rhoda Maddison reached the foot of the stairs. Rhoda glanced at them, at the ashen features of Rose Cromwell, and ran down the cellar steps.

Robinson and the sergeant followed her. She created no scene. She looked at her brother's body, and at the arrow in the cupboard door. Then she put one hand to her throat, and said softly: "So he got there first!"

The sergeant nodded significantly to Robinson. It was a remark to remember.

"I think we'd better go back upstairs now, ma'am," he said, "I'll come up and 'phone the Inspector."

Rhoda sighed, and walked past him. She was consequently the first to reach the telephone, and although he protested at her use of it, she merely ignored him and rang Captain Saunders.

"Harry," she said in a steady voice, "Michael's been found dead in the cellar. Your arrows."

She rang off, and the sergeant stepped forward, but she dialled a Maunsby number. "Miss Gillian Maddison, please. It's urgent."

The sergeant fretted beside her.

"Gillian? You'd better come home, dear. Michael's dead."

She almost threw the receiver back on its rest, as if she had no further use for it—ever. She walked into the kitchen, and filled and plugged in the kettle.

"Gawd! She's as hard as bleeding nails," said Robinson as he watched her go.

"She's a lady, and that's something you wouldn't under-stand," said the sergeant as he dialled his number.

"And you would, of course," muttered Robinson.

The sergeant covered the mouthpiece with his hand. "I'll remember that one day, my lad! What I meant, you thickhead, was that she's a proper lady, trained not to show her feelings!"

"Pity she wasn't trained same way with her legs," said Robin-son. "Dunno how they support her!"

"The pub does that," retorted the sergeant, and removed his hand to make the call.

Inspector Lancaster, of the Maunsby C.I.D. was the first to arrive, fifteen minutes later, bringing with him his sergeant, MacFarlane, and a train of assistants. The police sergeant and Robinson accompanied him down the cellar, where he exam-ined Maddison's body and then scratched his head.

"Can't even remember reading about a job like this," he com-plained. "The arrow point has gone straight through him!"

He was a man of medium height, with brown hair and brown eyes, a friendly man so ordinary in appearance that he passed in any crowd as anything but a detective.

"There's a name on the arrow," said the sergeant.

"Mine," said a voice behind them. Captain Saunders walked to them and knelt on the cellar floor. "A perfect gold, straight through the centre of the target. Whoever did this knew how to handle a bow!"

"How did you get here?" demanded Lancaster. "Well, you're here, so what did you mean by that last remark?"

"It's a hunting arrow, and the point of balance is well forward. The heavy pile, or point, obviously makes it tend to fall more in flight than a normal arrow. Any novice would have hit the floor, or at least hit Maddison lower in the body."

"Miss Maddison said the arrows were yours," the sergeant interrupted.

Saunders nodded. "Yes, they are mine. They were stolen a few days ago."

"How, where, and when?" demanded Lancaster.

Saunders told the whole story.

"So they were taken from behind the bar on a busy night?"

"That's it," said Saunders. He got to his feet, and stood at ease, his legs apart, his hands clasped behind his back.

"When did you last see Maddison?" asked Lancaster.

"Four—no, five nights ago. I've been to London on business."

"We'll have a chat later," said Lancaster. "You may be able to help me with the technical angle." He nodded toward the steps. "You might see if the doctor has arrived, please."

Saunders took the hint and went back to the ground floor of the inn and through to the kitchen. Rhoda was brewing tea. "Have a cup, Harry?" she asked evenly.

"Thanks," said Saunders. He looked hard at her. She was as neat and tidy as if ready for a trip into town. The black hair was smoothed over her head, and away from her uncreased forehead. The bun at the nape of her neck looked artificial and machine-made in its perfection. Her grey eyes were steady, and her features expressionless. Apart from a slight pinching of the aquiline nose there was no sign to indicate the shock she must have received.

"Rotten bad show," Saunders mumbled. "Who on earth hated him *so* much?"

"Those who live by the sword . . ." Rhoda said with an ironic and whimsical half-smile. "One of his hates must have caught up with him. Funny, you know . . ."

"What's funny?" Saunders asked brusquely.

She glanced toward the open doorway, and lowered her voice. "I was going to do it myself, in the same manner, in another week. It was all planned."

"Rhoda!" exclaimed Saunders. "Not that! Not you!"

"Why not?" she asked easily. "I owed him nothing, and he was in the way, you know!"

"Good God!" said Saunders.

Rhoda gave him a mocking smile. "Never mind! Someone has saved me the trouble. It wasn't you, Harry . . . ?"

Saunders pulled his upper lip between his teeth. "I'll kill in war, Rhoda, but be hanged to cold-blooded killing for no earthly reason!"

"I didn't expect you to admit it," she replied softly, "but thanks all the same! The way is clear now."

"Rhoda!" Saunders protested.

"Perhaps it was our little Gillian," smiled Rhoda. "Staying in town with Sally would make a nice alibi—and she did hate him, you know!"

"Sally—" began Saunders, and suddenly closed his mouth, very tightly.

Rhoda continued to smile at him in a secret manner. "Close the door, Harry. We must talk about this thing."

He shook his head as if to clear it of uncomfortable thoughts, closed the door, and turned with puzzled eyes.

"There's a thing we must do," said Rhoda. "We've all three benefited by Michael's death, and whichever of us killed him has well served the turn of the other two. That is a debt that must be repaid, and so on no account must the guilty person be trapped by the police. We'll invent a mystery man of whom Michael was afraid—some man from his past, and that will explain why he came to a quiet little village like this . . ." Saunders shook his wondering head from side to side. Rhoda handed him a cup of tea. "A pure fiction, of course, but we must keep it up. We mustn't volunteer the information, but let the police drag it from us reluctantly. Then they can chase their own tails. We must all three stick together."

Saunders had by now recovered his mental balance. He drew a chair up to the table, sat across it with his arms spread across its back, and wagged a finger at Rhoda.

"Now listen, Rhoda! Before we go any further, I did not kill Michael, for you or myself, so get that into your head! Secondly, I don't think Gillian capable of such a foul and dirty act, and unless you killed him yourself there really must be a mystery man in the background."

"You think I'm capable, Harry?"

"You've admitted it!"

"Ye-es, so I have. That was a mistake. I really meant doing it early this morning, and then postponed it for a week. It suddenly occurred to me that it would look bad for me if I was the only other person in the house—Gillian was staying in Maunsby . . ."

"I didn't know that," murmured Saunders.

"By the way," Rhoda smiled, "I saw you come home last night! I watched your car-lights from the attic window."

"A taxi," said Saunders. "Yes, I came straight home after ringing you. The driver was champing his bit outside the call-box. But I didn't think I was coming home to this."

"Well, that's the plan," said Rhoda. "I'll coach Gillian before the police get at her."

She took a deep breath, and sighed. "Anyway, the opposition has been removed!"

Saunders sniffed. "Hardly the time to talk of such things!"

"Why not? I didn't love him. Like my father and mother, he thought I was on earth merely to pander to him, to wait and to serve. I'm going to live for the first time in my life, Harry! This place is making money now, so we'll keep it on. We'll get Roberts back, and I'll manage the place—unless you'd like to do it!"

Saunders drew the cup and saucer toward him and sipped the tea, keeping his eyes down. He never had liked people, particularly women, who did his planning for him.

There came a knock on the door, and Inspector Lancaster walked in. Rhoda immediately got up and fetched another cup and saucer from the cupboard.

"Notice any unusual or suspicious characters in the place last night, Miss Maddison?" Lancaster asked.

"No-o, I can't say that I did, Inspector. Just the regulars so far as I remember."

"See anyone hanging around the side door for any length of time?"

"No. A cup of tea, Inspector?"

"Thank you," said Lancaster. "Miss Cromwell tells me she heard a queer click when she opened the door this morning, and we've found the reason. A piece of celluloid has been fixed over the latch-box. The plate has been unscrewed, the celluloid cut to shape, and screwed behind the plate so that the catch couldn't engage. When the door was closed, and the latch free, it would appear to be safely locked, but whoever wanted to get in had only to push the door—as Miss Cromwell did this morning."

"That looks as if someone had *planned* to get in and kill my brother!" said Rhoda.

"It would seem so," said Lancaster.

Rhoda gave a sigh of relief. "I'm glad of that. There was only myself in the house with Michael, and it might have looked as if—as if—you know!"

"That is so," said Lancaster. "At what time did your brother usually rise, Miss Maddison?"

"About seven-thirty as a rule, Inspector. He'd had to start rising early. He sacked the cellarman in a fit of temper, and consequently had to do his work as well as his own."

Lancaster raised an eyebrow. "This was generally known, Miss Maddison?"

Rhoda hesitated. "Well, all the village knew Roberts had been sacked. Actually, he walked out after a quarrel with my brother, so we can take it for granted that anyone who knew anything about the running of an inn would know Michael was doing his work."

"I see," said Lancaster, rubbing his cheek. "What was the quarrel about?"

"It was my brother's fault entirely," Rhoda assured him. "He was in a temper over something or other, and accused Roberts of not doing his work efficiently. As a matter of fact he said the beer was too heady. In fairness to Roberts, I'll say it was not! He was a good cellarman. He took umbrage, and I don't blame him. My brother could be a wee bit difficult to get on with!"

Lancaster turned to Saunders. "The arrows vanished before or after Roberts left the inn?"

"They were missed afterwards, Inspector."

"It was after," said Rhoda. "I remember Michael was handling the tap-room pumps, taking Roberts' place, and I went to him to ask if he had moved the arrows—Captain Saunders was ready for going home."

"That's correct," said Saunders.

"You didn't see Roberts come back in the house?"

"No."

"Where does he live?"

"About forty yards up the road, on the opposite side. Ninety-seven is the number of the house."

Lancaster turned back to Saunders. "The arrows, Captain Saunders; how would you describe them?"

"Technically?" asked Saunders. "Well, the one that killed him is a bodkin-pointed hunting arrow, and the one that was apparently shot at him and missed is a spear-headed hunting arrow. They belong to sets I had made for chasing small game, but have never used."

Lancaster mumbled something to himself. "You had them made? By whom?"

"Len Cowan. He lives across at Brookdale, and is one of the best bowyers and fletchers in the country. I had seven of each."

"I'd like your expert opinion," said Lancaster. "Do you think they were used as stabbing weapons, or shot from a bow?"

Saunders smiled. "I'm thinking about the one in the door. You wouldn't miss so badly if using them as swords, surely!"

"Quite a point!" murmured Lancaster.

"They were shot," went on Saunders. "At forty-five yards, drawn in a forty or forty-five pound bow, they're quite capable of going through—well, at sixteen yards. I've put one of them clean through a box target I made! It was faced with one-sixteenth copper sheet, backed with three-eighths plaster board, and the three-inch space between was filled with tightly-packed straw."

Lancaster whistled softly. "I shouldn't have thought the wooden shafts would have stood up to it."

"They are alloy, Inspector, anodised wood-yellow. It's obvious you haven't handled them yet."

"True," said Lancaster. "It would be possible to draw a bow in the cellar—enough top room?"

Saunders considered the matter before replying: "Yes, the ceiling is high enough. What do you think, Rhoda?"

"I think so, yes."

"You're an archer, Miss Maddison?" Lancaster asked quickly.

"A member of Captain Saunders' club."

"How many members have you, Captain?"

"Twenty men and six ladies."

"That's going to make matters much easier!" Lancaster said ironically.

Gillian ran into the room, glancing anxiously at each of them in turn, and finally grabbing Rhoda's hands. "What's happened? Where's Michael? Was he ill?"

Rhoda, leaning idly against the table, looked calmly into the frightened blue eyes. "Michael has been murdered, Gillian, with Harry's arrows."

She caught Gillian as she was swaying. Lancaster nodded to Saunders, and together they walked out of the room and to the street.

"Know anything about this Roberts?" Lancaster asked.

"Enough to know he didn't kill Maddison. He's a friendly little fellow with a red humorous face, and a bit of a tummy. He'd no need to kill Maddison. He walked straight into another job, so had no motive there. No, as a man who's been used to dealing with men all my life I'll say he isn't a murderer. Just not the type."

Lancaster grunted. "We've heard that before."

"He can't handle a bow," said Saunders.

"It isn't easy to use a bow?" asked Lancaster. "Couldn't any amateur take one and a couple of arrows and plug a man at short distance?"

"Archery's a skill and an art," said Saunders. "I doubt if you could hit a four-feet target from ten yards with your first dozen arrows."

"Not so good," said Lancaster. "You insist that an experienced archer killed Maddison?"

"I'll stick to that."

"And you've twenty-six members in your club!"

"Like a list of them?"

"A nice suggestion," said Lancaster. "When can I have it?"

"Now, if you care to come down to my house. It's only a few minutes away."

Lancaster led the way to his parked car. On the way to Ellwood House he asked more questions.

"Know of anybody else who held a grudge against Maddison?"

"No, I can't say that I do."

"I'm thinking of that door, now," said Lancaster. "It's on the blind side of the house—doesn't face any other houses, and is behind a buttress. Is it much used?"

"Yes and no," replied Saunders. "It was purposely built in that position. Maddison had the place turned inside out when he came two years ago. He had a club-room made over the front porch. Knowing there are always a number of teetotallers in village clubs, he and the architect arranged for the stairs to be in that lobby, and the door where it is, so's they could get in and out without being seen by the regulars."

"The hatch in the short end of the bar?"

"Only in use when there's a meeting on upstairs. The drinking members can have a quick one without having to go into the main part of the house."

"How many clubs in the village?"

"Well now, let me think. There's a fur-and-feather club, a pig club, two death-and-dividing clubs, the dart club, and the Buffs, and our archery club, the cricket club, the—"

"Lay off, please," sighed Lancaster. "You make it worse with every question you answer!"

"We're here, anyway," said Saunders. "Turn through the gateway on your right."

He took Lancaster into the house and set him up with two fingers of whisky, and then led him to the archery room in the west wing.

Lancaster looked round at the bows and the arrow-racks. "The bows are big things to carry around, aren't they? The fellow would have to approach in pitch darkness to get in without being prominent."

Saunders smiled. "Not necessarily."

He took one of the bows and pulled the limbs apart. The lower four inches of the upper-limb was metal sheathed, and fitted into a metal-lined socket in the lower limb.

"Take-apart bows, Inspector, especially designed to save the poking-out of eyes on buses and trains."

"Interesting. Really something!" murmured Lancaster. "You have some kind of carrying-case?"

Saunders flicked a long green baize bag from a shelf. "This is what I use. If you want to be posh and county there are cases designed to take bow, arrows, and everything but your shaving kit, but I find them bulky and prefer this kind of thing. It's just a bag with a row of stitches down the middle to divide it and so prevent the two limbs rubbing on each other."

Lancaster was staring at the arrows. "Not all the same length?"

"Oh no! Depends on the length of one's arms. The way to measure for arrows is stretch both arms in front of you like this, palms open and fingertips touching. You then measure from the tips to the point of the chin. Actually, that's a debatable point among archers. Some measure from the throat. Anyway, I use a twenty-seven inch arrow."

"How many of the hunting arrows did you say you had made?"

"Seven of each. I had two pairs of each made, and then an extra one of each."

Lancaster squinted at him. "I know I'm not too hot on arithmetic, Captain Saunders, but really . . ."

Saunders laughed. "Sorry! In archery three arrows make a pair—a prince's pair is the actual term."

"The list, please," said Lancaster, and when Saunders produced it he glanced through it and put it in his wallet. "You won't mind if I call again to ask you questions about archery?"

"Anything I can do," Saunders shrugged. "I liked Maddison."

"Know much about him?"

"Hardly anything," said Saunders, "although I could never understand why a man of his intelligence buried himself in a village like Teverby."

"He was well-educated?"

"I'd say yes to that."

"Population of Teverby's about three thousand, isn't it?"

"About that, yes."

"You don't think he was—well, hiding?"

"Candidly, I don't know what to think," said Saunders. "Well, if you are going perhaps you'll take my man with you as far as the inn. I left my car there."

Lancaster went straight back to his headquarters, from where he held a long telephone conversation with his superiors. He felt easier in his mind when he replaced the receiver. The Chief Constable had decided to ask Scotland Yard for assistance while the case, if not the body of Michael Maddison, was still warm.

At eight o'clock that night he met Gordon Knollis off the London train, and hurried him to his office to acquaint him with the details of the case.

CHAPTER V

THE ELEMENTARY DEDUCTIONS

RHODA MADDISON wasn't at all sure that she liked Inspector Gordon Knollis. He was a greying man in a grey suit, with grey eyes that looked down along an inquisitive nose. He sat on the edge of a chair in the sitting-room of the Fox, as relaxed and dispassionate as a schoolmaster asking questions in elementary mental arithmetic of a junior class. He smiled assuringly from time to time as he listened to Rhoda's story, nodding as she emphasised certain points, and interrupting occasionally when a statement needed clarifying. He was far too satisfied with her story, and she would have felt more comfortable if he had attempted to bully her. He was just too smooth.

His apparent satisfaction was too suspicious, because she could not concentrate. Gillian was sitting opposite, in a cream blouse and brown skirt, and she was wearing a thin gold chain round her neck, one Rhoda had not seen before. Something, very obviously, was hanging from it, and whatever it was it was not visible, being concealed within her bosom. An uneasy feeling was worrying Rhoda, and she would not be happy until she had proved or disproved it. Gillian usually took a malted-milk drink before going to bed, and in the secret drawer in the bureau was a tiny box containing a number of one-grain pheno-barbitone tablets. When Gillian was safely asleep, Knollis's crisp voice broke into her reverie. "So you went to bed about ten or fifteen minutes after midnight, Miss Maddison?"

Inspector Lancaster was lolling against the window at the far side of the room, behind Gillian, studying her answers and Knollis's methods.

Rhoda patted the bun at the nape of her neck, and nodded. "Yes, Inspector."

"You evidently slept heavily," said Knollis, "due to your late retirement. At what time do you usually retire?"

"Elevenish."

"Your brother, you say, has been in the habit of bringing a morning cup of tea to your bedroom?"

"Yes, he brought a cup to each of us."

"You never heard him get up this morning? Do you usually?"

"Oh yes!" Rhoda said.

"Michael was a banger-about," said Gillian. "He couldn't move quietly if he tried."

"How long did the cellar-work take?"

"About an hour a day, generally. Empty barrels have to be taken off, new ones put on, and then crates of empty bottles taken from the bar, and full ones taken up."

"Your brother had been going to bed at a normal hour? Say, elevenish, as in your own case?"

Rhoda paused for a moment, and then replied: "Well, no! He'd taken to sitting up late. Last night he made a start on the half-yearly accounts—tidying them so they wouldn't take so long at the end of the month."

"I'd like to look at the cellar again," said Knollis. "Perhaps you'll both come with us?"

Rhoda had no choice but to lead the way, Gillian brought up the rear, nervously determined not to be left alone in any part of the house.

"Inspector Lancaster tells me that alterations have been carried out," said Knollis when they reached the cellar. "With what object?"

Rhoda glanced at Gillian for support. "We honestly don't know what Michael had in mind, Inspector. He said the knocking of the two cellars into one would help the delivery-men and the cellar work in general."

"Has it done so?"

"Well, we can't see that it has, but one didn't argue with Michael," Rhoda replied with a shrug.

"Michael didn't answer questions," Gillian said. The tone in which she spoke made Knollis give her a second glance.

"The cupboard?" murmured Knollis. "What is kept in it, please?"

"We've never seen inside it, Inspector, believe me or not. I thought it was intended for a spirit-store, but the bottles are still racked in the next cellar."

"Considering the manner of your brother's death, and the peculiar location of it," said Knollis, "you can surely guess what might be in it?"

Lancaster raised an enquiring eyebrow. Knollis was away in front of him, let alone the two women.

"I'd like the key," said Knollis.

"I've never seen that, either, Inspector!"

Lancaster put his hand in his pockets. "I've got Mr. Maddison's keys, Knollis. They were in his hip pocket."

Knollis nodded, and Lancaster found the correct key and opened the doors.

A large cork bathmat was screwed to the wall, occupying most of the space in the cupboard. Fastened to it was a dartboard from which the wire frame and numbers had been removed, the centre of it being breast-high from the floor. Propped in one corner of the cupboard was a braced bow.

"Private archery practice!" exclaimed Lancaster.

"That's it!" said Knollis quietly.

"But why down here?" demanded Gillian. "There was the field. He could have used that!"

"This, of course, explains the alterations and his early rising and late retiring," said Knollis.

"He should have known better than to leave the bow braced," said Rhoda, clicking her tongue.

"Why?" asked Knollis.

"The bow is left under tension, and consequently strained."

"There's a point," said Lancaster. "There are no arrows to be found. Was he practising with the two hunting arrows only?"

He looked at Rhoda. There was a frown on her usually bland forehead. "I don't know what to think," she said.

"You've no idea who took the arrows on the night Captain Saunders missed them?" asked Knollis.

"Not—" Rhoda began, and then stopped.

"Not what, Miss Maddison?"

"Not unless he took them himself," she said slowly. "Michael, I mean, not Captain Saunders."

"I've seen the statement you made to Inspector Lancaster regarding the Roberts affair," said Knollis. "Do you think your brother could have picked up the arrows and concealed them when he followed Roberts to the lobby?"

"I suppose he could have done," Rhoda said vaguely. "That could be one explanation."

Knollis narrowed his eyes, and stared through the two women. "You have other arrows in the house?"

"I've a dozen and a half," said Rhoda.

"My dozen are in my wardrobe," replied Gillian.

"I see—e," Knollis said slowly.

Rhoda tried to get behind his eyes, but the man was impenetrable—and impossible. Whatever he saw he was keeping to himself.

He took them back to the ground floor of the inn, and left them all standing aimlessly in the lobby while he walked round the public rooms. He came back to the lobby and glanced round it.

"Who plays golf?" he asked, nodding to the bag hanging behind the swing door.

"Michael did occasionally," said Rhoda. "He hadn't played for several months. He seemed to have lost interest."

"He was a member of the archery club?" asked Knollis, and immediately added: "No, of course he wasn't!"

Rhoda shook her head. "He never showed any interest, other than in the two hunting arrows after the argument between Captain Saunders and Major Oliver."

Knollis pushed his hands into his jacket pockets, and sighed. "This lobby is cleaned every day?"

"Naturally, Inspector!"

"Your brother didn't take to staying up late and rising early until after the cellar alterations were completed? Is that a correct deduction?"

Gillian flashed a quick glance at her aunt, who grimaced.

"That is correct?" Knollis repeated.

"That—yes, that will be correct, Inspector."

"So we can assume that, on the night of the quarrel with Roberts he went to bed at the usual time—elevenish?"

"Ye-es, I think that is so, Inspector."

"Who cleans the lobby?"

"Rose Cromwell—one of my helps."

"She's still on the premises?"

"Yes. We're later tonight with all—this."

She looked up at the clock. It was twenty minutes to eleven.

"I'd like to speak to her," said Knollis.

Gillian went to find her. While she was away, Knollis asked: "This Miss or Mrs. Cromwell? Is she thorough?"

Rhoda shrugged. "Like all the rest of them, Inspector, she's thorough providing she is watched."

Rose Cromwell bustled in behind Gillian.

"You clean this lobby, Miss Cromwell?" asked Knollis.

"Yes sir. It's my first job every morning."

"You always dust the golf bag, of course!"

Rose wiped her hands down her full hips, and ran her tongue over her lips. Knollis watched the betraying actions, and smiled.

"You know what I'm going to ask you, don't you, Miss Cromwell?" he ventured.

She bobbed respectfully. "I think so, sir."

"Let's have it then," smiled Knollis. "There's nothing that can hurt anyone."

"It was the morning after the arrows went, sir. I found them in that bag. It was the green feathers that caught my eye."

"You didn't mention them to anyone?"

"It wasn't my business, sir," she said nervously. "I reckoned Mr. Maddison perhaps didn't want anybody to know they were there."

"He didn't," Rhoda said caustically.

"I thought he might have put them there for a joke," Rose Cromwell added.

"Michael had a marvellous sense of humour," said Rhoda.

"He saw jokes by appointment," added Gillian.

Knollis looked quickly at the two women. It was evident that neither of them had loved him very deeply.

"And they were gone the next morning, sir," Rose Cromwell said.

"You didn't think to ask Mr. Maddison about them?"

"Michael didn't answer questions," said Gillian for the second time that night.

"I expected you to say they had gone by the next day," said Knollis. "Thanks, that will be all, Miss Cromwell."

"How did you reach that remarkable conclusion?" Rhoda asked when Rose had gone.

"Nothing remarkable about it," said Knollis. "No other solution was possible. It seems credible to suggest that someone on the business side of the bar removed the arrows, and that means either yourself, your niece, or your brother. Your brother appears to be the only one who got away from the bar during the rush of custom, and if he went to the lobby he had to find a hiding place for the arrows. The bag is the only conceivable place. I've been told that Roberts went to the kitchen for his cap and jacket, and I'm suggesting it was then your brother put his hand round the door and took the arrows, slipping them among the golf clubs before Roberts got back from the kitchen. The deduction is elementary, but the question of why he took them is a different matter so far."

Rhoda smoothed the grey silk dress over her thighs, and looked down at the tiled floor of the lobby. "I see, Inspector. Yes, it is all perfectly clear when explained in that way."

"Who was he planning to kill, Miss Maddison?" Knollis asked suddenly.

He turned to Gillian. "Who *was* he planning to kill?"

Gillian moved nearer to her aunt, a fact which did not escape Knollis. Rhoda bit her lip. "What do you mean, Inspector?"

"Just what I asked," said Knollis. "Who was he planning to kill?"

"The idea is preposterous!"

"Michael didn't *kill* people," said Gillian.

Knollis noted the distinction and stored it in his mind. If he didn't kill people, what else did he do that wasn't exactly to his credit?

"The idea is preposterous," repeated Rhoda.

"In which case I don't know my job," Knollis returned crisply. "Miss Maddison, if your brother had been interested in archery, as such, he could have joined the club. We'll assume he was self-conscious and didn't want to make a fool of himself while learning, and so he had the cellar enlarged so that he could practice in secrecy. Nothing wrong there apart from the fact that he went to a deuce of a lot of trouble. He could have used your arrows, or Miss Gillian's, or he could have bought a set—"

He broke off, and smiled knowingly at her. "The bow in the cellar cupboard? Who does it belong to?"

"I—I don't know, Inspector. It isn't mine, and it isn't Gillian's. He must have bought it. It looks about his height."

"A point," interrupted Knollis. "I believe I am right in saying that one chooses a bow whose length is appropriate to one's height?"

"That's so," said Gillian. "I had a quick glance at the one down there, and it would be just right for Michael. The details are stamped on the upper limb, you know, and it's a five-feet six, drawing forty-five pounds at twenty-eight."

"Which means, in non-archery English," said Rhoda, "that when a twenty-eight inch arrow is drawn in it you have forty-five pounds behind it."

"Thank you," said Knollis. "Now my point is that if he bought a bow, why didn't he buy a set of arrows at the same time? Couldn't he buy arrows from the bowsmith?"

"The bow is by Len Cowan of Brookdale," said Gillian. "He's a fletcher as well as a bowyer, so Michael could have got them if he had needed them."

"That's it, then," said Knollis. "Why didn't he buy normal target arrows instead of stealing two genuinely lethal ones? Captain Saunders' hunting arrows are heavier than target arrows? Is that correct?"

Both Rhoda and Gillian nodded silently.

"In other words," said Knollis, "he saw no point in practising with normal arrows when he intended to use the two hunting arrows! He practised with those he intended to use! You do see what I'm getting at, Miss Maddison? That your brother had gone to all this trouble solely to practise for some criminal purpose."

"I—I—" Rhoda faltered.

Knollis put one foot on the regulating cock of the gold-painted radiator, and rested his hand on his knee.

"You see, Miss Maddison, we are trained to think logically, I'm now assuming that your brother was after someone, or someone was after him. I believe the first case to be the truth, otherwise why should he choose what is a more or less silent weapon?"

Rhoda stared past him to the wall. "Oh, my God, but this is horrible!"

"Tell me, Miss Maddison," said Knollis. "Is it true that Captain Saunders and yourself are to be married?"

A peculiar expression flitted over Gillian's pretty face. She covered it by fluffing her hair with both hands, and stroking her fingers across her tired eyes.

"Yes, oh yes!" Rhoda said more quickly than was necessary.

"Your brother was opposed to the marriage?"

"He was—yes!"

"Why?" Knollis asked abruptly.

Rhoda's hand crept to her throat and fingered the neck of her grey dress. "Michael liked to be the originator of ideas, and intensely disliked having to fall in with those of other people."

"Hardly a cogent reason," murmured Knollis. "Sure there was no more to it than that?"

She remained silent, while Gillian appeared to be interested only in her finger-nails.

Knollis sighed, and then excused himself while he ran down to the cellar again. On his return to the ground floor he said goodnight, and led the way outside to Lancaster's car.

"Well?" said Lancaster, breaking three-quarters of an hour's silence.

"Captain Saunders next, please," replied Knollis.

"It's turned eleven, you know!"

"The man isn't likely to be abed yet," said Knollis. "We can try the house. I'd rather like to see him tonight, if at all possible."

Lancaster was startled when he saw Knollis and Saunders together. Knollis was the elder by a few years, but otherwise there were few points which could not be matched when comparing them side by side. Both were of the same height, and carried themselves upright and somewhat stiffly. Both walked briskly, and talked with a crispness that could be mistaken for brusqueness. If Knollis had worn a moustache they might have been taken for brothers.

"We want information and ideas," said Knollis, and frankly told Saunders what had been found in the cellar.

"Queer that," said Saunders. "I half-suspected him of pinching my arrows, but couldn't find any logical reason why he should have done so. It didn't make sense. Private practice, eh? Now what the deuce . . . ?"

"Who was he planning to kill?" Knollis asked directly. "And why did he want to kill him?"

Saunders shrugged, and evaded Knollis's eyes. "I can't answer either question, Inspector. Honestly, I don't know!"

"He'd opposed your projected marriage to Miss Rhoda Maddison?"

Saunders took a hemp bowstring from his pocket and played with it.

"Yes, that is so. Miss Maddison told you that?"

"Of course. What was the objection?"

"Dunno," Saunders said shortly. "He merely said it wasn't convenient to his plans."

"You had a good talk about the matter?"

Saunders grimaced. "Actually, it wasn't about that at all. There'd been talk in the village about me making up to Miss Gillian. Maddison invited me into the sitting-room to tackle me about it. He wasn't against me wooing his sister—although even then I had to wait permission to marry her!—but drew the line completely if there was anything in the rumour about myself and Gillian. Quite definite about that!"

"Was there anything in the rumour?"

Saunders looked up from the bowstring and looked Knollis straight in the eyes. "Not a thing!"

"The arrows," said Knollis; "he could have bought a set similar to yours?"

"Oh yes! No difficulty about that!"

"You're satisfied that the two arrows found in the cellar are yours?"

"Absolutely satisfied—unfortunately."

"Would you say Maddison had it in for you? That he disliked you?"

"No, I'd say not. We got on pretty well together, as a matter of fact. Why do you ask?"

"I was wondering whether he stole your arrows so they wouldn't be traced back to him when he got his man, or whether he took them so that they'd be traced back to you after the same event had occurred."

"That's a pair of deucedly uncomfortable notions," said Saunders, "but I'll take the first if you don't mind."

"A question that I have to ask," said Knollis. "It's pure routine. Where were you in the early hours of this morning? You'll now tell me you were in bed!"

"I was," said Saunders. "I travelled back from London late last night, and didn't get into Maunsby until just before midnight, so I was ready for a good sleep. Got up about eight this morning. Anything else I can tell you?"

"Miss Rhoda Maddison led us to understand that a definite understanding exists between you. That correct?"

Saunders coughed, and glanced apologetically at Knollis and Lancaster in turn. "There are times when I could damn the woman. She's in too great a hurry. As a matter of fact, when Maddison tackled me about Gillian he was under the impression that I'd already proposed to Rhoda—and I hadn't. She either told him that directly, or led him to believe it. I didn't contradict him because I wanted time to think. Since Rhoda's had no notice to the contrary she's taken it for granted that I'm going to marry her."

"And you are not?"

Saunders sucked a tooth, and shook his head. "I'm not—but don't tell her yet!"

"Whether you do or not is nothing to do with us," said Knollis. "All we're seeking at the moment is possible motives for Maddison's death."

"Oh!"

Saunders raised his eyes.

"And wondering if she bumped him off because he came in between—good lord, man, you can't think that! It was obviously not her!"

"Why obviously?"

"The strip of celluloid over the latch-box!"

"Which could have been fitted just as easily by someone in the house as by a stranger, Captain Saunders!"

"That's true, I suppose," Saunders muttered.

"Many an inside job has been rigged to look like an outside one, and vice versa," said Knollis. "Anyway, I'm not suspecting anyone at present, but merely trying to find out who benefited by Maddison's death."

"Which lets me out," Saunders said quickly.

"How?" asked Knollis.

Saunders gave a wry smile. "Between we three men, I don't want to many her, and in that case Maddison objecting was of more value to me alive."

"She thinks you do want to marry her," said Knollis, "as if we haven't already been over this!"

"Er—yes."

"Why don't you tell her, and be done with it once and for all?"

"There'll be a scene, and I hate scenes, so I'm stalling as long as I can."

"What staff do you keep?" asked Knollis.

"My man, Alfred, and two girls. Milly—that's Miss Davidson, is my cook-housekeeper, and lives in. She and Alfred are getting married this autumn. The other girl, Ethel Burgoyne, lives in the village and comes in daily. Miss Davidson's on holiday in

Pembroke just now, and Ethel's down with a summer cold, or mild 'flu, or something similar, so Alfred and myself are living a bachelor life temporarily."

"They have their own side of the house, of course?"

"Oh yes, the east wing."

"And only trespass on this side in the course of their duties?"

"Lord, yes," said Saunders. "You can't have them taking liberties even in these democratic days. Must have some sort of discipline, you know!"

"I expected that answer," smiled Knollis. "Your army training, naturally."

"I suppose the place is run on something like service lines," Saunders grinned. "Alfred was my batman out East, so it works out all right. Habit, as you suggest. It makes for efficiency. Why do you ask, anyway?"

"I've a good mind to tell you," said Knollis. He waited a moment, smiled, and added: "But I won't!"

"Thanks for nothing," said Saunders.

"This rumour regarding Miss Gillian? How did it arise, Captain?"

"How do such rumours arise in a village?" Saunders asked rhetorically. "It's a lot of bunk, anyway. I'm interested in the girl as an archer, but no more. She's a natural. You don't have to teach her anything—well, not much. With just that extra bit of tuition and practice she'll be good enough to shoot against anyone in the country."

"So good?" murmured Knollis quietly. "Well, thanks, Captain Saunders, and now we must let you get to bed!"

When they were driving back to Maunsby along Woodstock Lane, Lancaster said: "I nearly forgot myself and challenged him. He's a liar, you know, if he says he got into town just before midnight. The London train lands at eleven-twenty—and that doesn't check with any of the facts we've learned about his movements."

"That's worth knowing," said Knollis.

"Why the question about the staff keeping their own quarters?" Lancaster asked curiously.

Knollis smiled in the darkness. "Saunders, as you say, is a liar. I noticed a brown beret and a pair of brown kid gloves on the chest in the hall—ladies' wear, Lancaster! That suggested either that his staff took liberties in the house—which I doubted, or that some lady was very much at home and could leave her stuff about even when not there. Now I can't imagine the somewhat prissy Miss Rhoda wearing a brown beret. . . . !"

"They wear green ones when arching, or archering, or whatever they call it," said Lancaster. "You're probably right about Miss Rhoda, so that means Miss Gillian! And that in turn means there may be some truth in the rumour that came to Maddison's ears!"

There was silence but for the purring engine.

"And that may explain why he doesn't care to throw over Miss Rhoda openly and cleanly," added Lancaster.

"Exactly," said Knollis in a tone of deep satisfaction.

Chapter VI
THE LITTLE FOX

RHODA MADDISON watched Knollis and Lancaster go, and smiled wryly at Gillian. "We must stick together, dear. They'll do their best to prove that one of the three of us murdered Michael."

"Why on earth should they?" Gillian asked in a startled voice.

"Because one of us did," replied Rhoda, "and your guess is as good as mine. Oh well, we can't do ourselves or Michael any good by staying up all night, can we? I feel really jaded. I think I'll take a drink with you tonight. You rest while I prepare it. See, is it two spoonfuls of your malted milk food you take?"

"I'll do it," said Gillian. "You've had a heavier day than myself."

"I'll make it," Rhoda said firmly, and went through to the kitchen. While the milk was warming in the saucepan she wandered through to the sitting-room. She was looking in the bureau, balancing the drop-panel against her thin bosom when Gillian followed her into the room.

Rhoda looked round quickly. "This is a job we'll have to do shortly, dear, and I hate starting it—Michael's papers, I mean. Oh well!"

She let the panel drop back into place and went back to the kitchen. Gillian watched her go, her eyes fixed on Rhoda's right fist. It didn't make sense, only one fist clenched. It looked as if she was holding something.

Gillian moved to the bureau and looked inside, then pressed the tiny catch that released the secret drawer. It slid open. Inside was a small pasteboard pillbox. On its label was written: *The Tablets. Pheno-Barbitone. Take three at bed-time.*

There was a chance that Rhoda was going to take them herself, but it didn't seem likely. Aunt Rhoda objected to taking pills, and would not even swallow a single aspirin when she had a headache. The tablets had been prescribed for Michael when he had a nasty cycle accident some six months ago, but he preferred a nightcap from the bar. And she had seen Rhoda's eyes on the thin gold chain round her neck. It was obvious!

She took three of the tablets from the box, slipped them into the pocket of her nigger skirt, and closed the drawer and the bureau. She tiptoed to the door and pushed it to before dialling a number on the telephone that stood on the bureau.

"Harry dear? I can't explain now, but in exactly four minutes I want you to give Aunt Rhoda a ring, and I want her out of the way for at least three minutes! Oh, you'll think of something! And then you can slip in after midnight. The celluloid is still in place. 'Bye, darling!"

She walked slowly back to the kitchen, where Rhoda was pouring milk into two beakers.

"Were you on the 'phone?" Rhoda asked without looking up from the beakers.

Gillian shook her head warily. "I went all fainty and had to grab the bureau. Perhaps I knocked the 'phone. I don't know."

Rhoda helped her to a chair. "You're tired, darling. It's the reaction setting in. Sip your drink slowly and go to bed. You'll feel better after a good night's sleep."

She handed a beaker to Gillian, and leaned against the refrigerator with her own in her hand, sipping it slowly. The telephone bell jangled through the house, and Gillian began to rise.

"I'll go dear," Rhoda said quickly. "Probably Harry—for me!"

Gillian watched her hurry away, and then tipped Rhoda's milk into the saucepan, and her own milk into Rhoda's beaker. She refilled her own beaker from the saucepan, and, the exchange made, tipped the three tablets into Rhoda's drink and rinsed the saucepan. When Rhoda returned she was lolling in the chair, her head tipped back and resting against the wall.

"It was Harry!" Rhoda said triumphantly. "Your milk will be getting cold, dear!"

Gillian shook herself, and blinked. "I nearly went off then. Yes, I'd better get to bed."

She finished the malted milk drink, put the beaker on the stainless-steel draining-board, and covered her mouth as she yawned widely. She said goodnight to her aunt, and went up the stairs. She arranged her bedroom to her satisfaction, changed, and got into bed, switching off the bed-light.

A quarter of an hour elapsed, and a thin strip of light appeared down the edge of the door.

"Gillian. Gillian darling!"

Gillian stirred and snuggled deeper into the pillows. Seen through slitted lids, Rhoda didn't look any too good now she was washed. Her cheeks were pale, and there were dark rings round her eyes. Her movements were slow, and almost forced.

She tiptoed to the bed. "Gillian!" she whispered.

Her long hand moved inside the sheets, felt round Gillian's neck, and then explored between her breasts. The sheets were drawn up again, and Rhoda went over to the dressing-table. Gillian waited, a light smile on her lips.

"A crucifix! Well . . ."

Rhoda gave a long and audible sigh of relief.

The door closed again. Gillian opened her eyes, and listened. She heard the key turn in Rhoda's door. She lay for another quarter of an hour, until the church clock chimed the quarter after midnight, and then got up and put on her wrap and slippers. She crept into the corridor and down the stairs, returning a few minutes later with a clothes-line. Working in the darkness, she made a running noose in one end of it, and slipped it over the handle of Rhoda's door. She felt round and tied an overhand loop knot round the pipe that fed the radiator opposite. The rest of the line she led past her own doorway. Then she went downstairs.

The rest of the story was Rhoda's, as told to Knollis and Lancaster at eight o'clock the next morning. She slept heavily that night, more heavily than she could remember sleeping before. She was so heavy-eyed when she awoke that she made for the bathroom to sluice the sleep from her head—only to find she could not open the door. It gave about a quarter of an inch when she tugged at the handle, and she realised it had been tied up from the corridor. She thumped on it to attract Gillian, but could get no reply. It was then seven-fifteen.

She sat on the edge of the bed for a few minutes while she tried to make her brain work, and wondered what to do. She then dressed and went to the window. Some men were cycling past to work, men she knew—patrons of the Fox. She called to them, and they tried to find a way in, but all the windows and doors were securely closed. She gave them permission to break a window, and this three of them did while the fourth went to the call-box down the road to telephone the police.

When the men got in they found a line tightly looped round her door-handle and tied to the radiator. It was then taken to Gillian's door, where it was again fastened. One of the men was a war-time special constable of some experience, and he had cut the line, leaving the knots for police examination.

"And Miss Gillian?" asked Knollis, looking across the sitting-room. "You slept heavily?"

"I'm still asleep," Gillian said wearily.

"We had to shake her quite roughly to wake her," said Rhoda. "When I came downstairs—well, you can see what had happened! The bureau has been completely rifled. Even the secret drawer was open."

"We made a mistake in not removing the celluloid from the latch-box," Knollis said wryly. "We must take responsibility for what has happened. You know it was removed in the night?"

Rhoda did not, although she said she had wondered why the men hadn't found the side door capable of being pushed open, and it wasn't until morning she remembered she had been sleeping in an unlocked house.

Knollis looked at the bureau. "We can assume that all evidence which might point to the murder has been taken away. What a gaffe we've made! You hadn't looked through your brother's papers by any chance, Miss Maddison?"

"I haven't had time to even think about them," said Rhoda, glancing askance at Gillian.

Knollis nodded, and leaned back on the settee, his hands planted flat on the upholstery. The little finger of his left hand came into contact with something smooth and hard. He cocked an eye at Lancaster and made a pretence of blowing his nose, and with his handkerchief in his left hand managed to cover the object and put it in his pocket. It felt very much like a cross.

"It looks as if someone knew the house very well," said Rhoda. "I mean, they found the secret drawer."

"I wouldn't infer that, Miss Maddison," said Knollis. "It's fair to assume that the maker of the bureau fitted the same type of secret drawer on all the bureaux he made. The word *secret* is deceptive in such cases."

"You're not too hopeful of finding who locked us in and robbed us?" Gillian asked in an unsteady voice.

Knollis watched her slowly for a few seconds, and then shook his head. "The sergeant says there are no prints in the room other than your own, your aunt's, and your late uncle's. Still, our man may have made a slip somewhere, so we'll go over the room again. You'll see to that, Inspector Lancaster?"

Lancaster nodded.

Knollis rose with a sigh and led the way back to the car. Lancaster followed him and slid under the wheel.

"Back up the road until we're out of sight from the inn windows," said Knollis. Then he took the handkerchief from his pocket and laid it on his knee, exposing a gold crucifix. "This was slipping down the back of the settee, Lancaster. Not the kind of thing a person mislays without searching for it pretty thoroughly, is it? Eighteen carat, too."

"Not necessarily significant, surely?" said Lancaster. "It obviously belongs to one of the women, but it doesn't prove that either of them were in that room, rifling it. They'd have a deuce of a job to rope the outside of a bedroom door from inside, anyway!"

"Just what I'm thinking," said Knollis ambiguously. "What was the name of Saunders' day-girl?"

"Burgoyne."

"You got her address?"

"Oh yes, she lives just up the road. Want to talk to her about something?"

"There's an idea stirring in my mind," said Knollis.

Ethel Burgoyne and her mother were not sure whether to be scared when Knollis and Lancaster went to the house, or whether to be elated because they would have something to tell the neighbours.

"Would you have been taking a holiday this week even if you had not caught this cold?" Knollis asked the weedy and adenoidal girl.

"It's 'flu, sir."

"Just as you wish," said Knollis, "but that doesn't answer my question."

"I was to have the week off, sir."

"How long ago was it arranged?"

"A month, sir. The Captain asked me if this week would suit me, and I said it would, so he gave me this week, sir."

"I'm slowly getting the idea," Knollis said sarcastically.

"I was going to see my cousin Mabel at Sheerness—"

"Thanks," said Knollis.

"What's this about?" Lancaster asked as they walked back down the village street to the car.

"Your information about the London train," Knollis replied. "If the train gets into Maunsby at eleven-twenty, and Saunders telephoned Miss Rhoda Maddison from Maunsby station at midnight—you see what I mean? It's only five miles from Teverby to Maunsby, along a good clear country road—Woodstock Lane. On the other hand we have the medical evidence to tell us that Maddison was murdered about half-past six the same morning. The time-factor doesn't help us with the murder, but it does help us when we think about another little matter which may prove relevant."

"What other little matter?" Lancaster asked.

"The crucifix."

Knollis took it out of his pocket and laid it on the palm of his hand. "You see, Lancaster, there are no breakages. The loop at the top of the cross is intact, as is the loose link which is threaded through it. In short, it hasn't been lost by slipping off whatever it was fastened to. It has been *taken off*!"

"Taken off what?"

They reached the car and got in. Knollis stared blankly through the windscreen, his eyes reduced to narrow slits.

"Little Miss Gillian wears a fine gold chain round her neck. It has some attraction for Miss Rhoda. She can't keep her eyes off it—or couldn't when we interviewed her last night."

Lancaster rubbed his chin with his knuckles. "I am not clairvoyant, so can't read your mind, Knollis!"

"I'm suggesting that she's taken this crucifix from the chain and put something else in its place. Now where did she spend her holiday?"

"Didn't she say Eastness?"

"Yes, that's right," Knollis nodded. "Now I want to see Miss Rhoda Maddison again."

Rhoda scowled as they walked in. She had enough to do, even with Gillian at home to help her, without having to keep breaking off to answer questions—most of which she couldn't answer.

Knollis would not allow Gillian to be present at this interview, and carefully closed the door of the sitting-room before turning to Rhoda with his first introductory remarks.

"I prefer privacy on this occasion," he said, "because this interview may prove a wee bit embarrassing for you. I want to ask some plain questions about Captain Saunders. My method is to eliminate those people who have been intimately connected with a deceased person, and then I can concentrate on those left."

He deliberately let a moment or so elapse, and then said subtly: "So I didn't want your niece to be present."

Rhoda sighed, almost happily.

"Captain Saunders went to London four days before your brother was killed?"

"Yes, Inspector. He was in London four days—no, three days, if you see what I mean!"

"I do," nodded Knollis. "Did he contact you at all while he was away—say by telephone?"

"Not by 'phone, but I had letters from him. The Englebert Hotel. I think, judging by the postmarks, it is in the West-One postal district."

"We've been into this before," said Knollis, "but he 'phoned you from Maunsby at midnight two nights ago, as soon as he stepped from the train?"

"Oh yes!"

"He came straight home?"

"Oh yes!" Rhoda said again.

"How do you know?" Knollis asked quickly. "Did he 'phone you again from home?"

Rhoda hesitated, and then gave an embarrassed smile.

"You'll think I'm no better than a silly girl, but I went to the attic and watched the lights of his car as he drove home along Woodstock Lane."

"Over the houses, Miss Maddison?"

"No. If you look across the road from the side door you'll see there's a gap between the houses. From the attic one can see the lane quite clearly."

"I understand," said Knollis. "What a pity he didn't come home via the main road, isn't it?"

Rhoda was startled. "The—the main road, Inspector?"

Knollis nodded easily. "He might have seen someone hanging about. You see, I'm wondering if someone entered the house very late, and lay hidden until your brother went down the cellar next morning."

"A most uncomfortable thought, Inspector!"

"Now for your niece. She had been on holiday?"

Rhoda began to look more at her ease now the subject was changing.

"Gillian? Yes, she'd been to Eastness. She rang me rather late from Maunsby and asked if she could stay the night with her friend, Sally Denby, and go straight to business from there in the morning, and return home during the evening. Sally also came on the 'phone, so I had no doubts in my mind at all."

"No—er—doubts?" Knollis asked softly.

Rhoda blinked rapidly and said: "I'd been worried at not seeing or hearing from her earlier in the evening. Once I knew where she was . . ."

"Why, of course!" said Knollis. "She did go to work from her friend's house?"

Rhoda was obviously puzzled by the question. "Well, naturally! She was there when I rang to tell her about Michael's death."

"That's all I have to ask you," said Knollis. "Your niece is in an office in Maunsby?"

"Hartley and Brown—they are the wine merchants in Northgate."

"Keeping in the trade, eh?" smiled Knollis.

He had Lancaster run him into Maunsby and to the offices of the wine merchants'. Here he asked for the manager.

"You have a Miss Sally Denby working here?"

"You want to see her?"

"Privately if possible. Can you oblige us?"

Miss Denby came nervously into the office, and looked alarmed when the manager closed the door and left her with the two detectives. Lancaster introduced himself and Knollis, and assured her that there was nothing to be afraid of. Privately, he didn't know what Knollis had in mind.

"You took your holiday at Eastness last week, Miss Denby?"

"Yes, sir."

"You went alone?"

"No, sir. I went with a friend."

"Can you give us his name, please?"

She looked shocked. "It was a girl friend, sir."

"Her name then?"

"Miss Gillian Maddison."

"You returned—when?"

"Sunday evening, sir."

"Getting into Maunsby at what time?"

"About five minutes to eleven. The train was a bit late."

"You returned from Eastness together, Miss Denby?"

"Oh yes, sir. Of course."

Knollis nodded. "Then what happened, Miss Denby?"

She flushed, and hesitated. "Why, we telephoned Jill's aunt—from my home—and she stayed all night with me."

"And you came on to business together the next morning, which was Monday?"

"Yes, sir! That's just it!"

Knollis smiled at her. "Sorry to put you about. Miss Maddison's uncle has been murdered, as you will know, and we have to check on all the statements made to us. Everything is all right now. Thanks for helping us so readily!"

The manager came in again as Sally Denby went out. Knollis reached for the telephone directory.

"Can you give me Miss Denby's home address?" he asked.

"I can get it from the files," said the manager. "Yes, here we are: 43 Canal Road."

Knollis turned the pages of the directory, and ran his finger down the Denbys. Then he asked permission to use the office telephone, and asked for Enquiries.

"I'm needing the number of a new subscriber who isn't in the current directory," he said. "The name is Denby, Forty-three Canal Road. Thank you."

He waited for a time, said his thanks again, and replaced the receiver.

"Not on, Lancaster," he said shortly. "That settles it!"

"What's it all about?" Lancaster pleaded as they plodded down the stairs to the street. "I'm completely in the darkness!"

"Dawn's breaking—on the minor matter," said Knollis.

"Who are we after?" Lancaster demanded, almost treading on Knollis's heels as he pressed for an answer.

"The fox," said Knollis.

"Back there again!"

"I don't mean the inn," said Knollis, "but the little fox who lives there. I mean the pretty, innocent little Miss Gillian. She did a neat and admirable piece of work."

"You mean she murdered her uncle? Are you sure? I'd got Rhoda lined up for that part."

"I don't know about the murder," said Knollis. "I wasn't thinking about it as a matter of fact. No, Miss Gillian apparently had the choice of life or death, and being wise in her generation, she chose life."

Lancaster snorted. "Now you're going cryptic and mystical! I am supposed to be helping to investigate this case, you know!"

Knollis paused on the pavement and gave Lancaster an apologetic smile. "I know! I know, Lancaster. I'm not ignoring you, even if it looks like it. It's just that I can't for the life of me express myself until I see the pattern of a theory making some sense. Let's get back to your office and clear the point, shall we?"

In Lancaster's office he used the telephone, while Lancaster sat by with slowly rising eyebrows.

"That's it, then," said Knollis as he turned away from the instrument. "Captain Harry Saunders and Miss Gillian Maddison were married by licence at All Saints' Church, Eastness, five days ago."

Lancaster thumbed a fill of tobacco into his pipe, and grunted. "H'm! So that cuts them out, and increases the odds against the aunt!"

Knollis smiled wryly. "I'm afraid Miss Rhoda is going to turn very nasty when she finds out, Lancaster. I hope Gillian has the sense to move into her husband's house. In fact I think we ought to drive her there, for her own safety."

CHAPTER VII
THE KNOLLIS RECONSTRUCTION

LANCASTER PUFFED slowly at his pipe, and cast quizzical glances at the sphinx-like Knollis on the other side of the wide office table. He was something new to Lancaster's experience. Here, in his own office, it was the practice to throw all the cards on the table and let any member of the staff comment on them, the underlying idea being that three or four heads were better than one. This Knollis man, while utterly likeable, was as companionable as a jilted girl at her rival's wedding. What he thought remained inside his own head until he considered the time was fully ripe to reveal it. That was all right, but it left Lancaster or whoever he had to work with on provincial cases too much in the dark. Lancaster felt he ought to be doing more, but he did not know what to do, and there was no chance of him taking a really active part in the investigation until Knollis decided to open up.

"This alters the whole aspect of the case," he said tentatively, in the hope of drawing Knollis.

Knollis continued to stare at the handle on the table drawer, and nodded. "It means the two letters Rhoda Maddison received from Saunders were posted for him by a London friend, and written before he went away. It means that all telephone calls she received were designed to remove suspicion and allow Gillian to spend the night with her husband at Elwood House. The Denby girl was lying—to orders. It means Gillian went to business from Teverby, and not from the Denby House . . ."

Lancaster grunted, and waited.

"Whose car did Rhoda really see from the attic?" asked Knollis.

"Sounds to me as if Saunders did the job thoroughly," said Lancaster. "But was he merely covering the marriage, or preparing the murder?"

"Let's sort this thing out," said Knollis, making ready to tick off the items on his long fingers. "Gillian goes to Eastness first.

Even with a special licence the couple are expected to give reasonable notice to the vicar or rector of the parish, so that covers that! Saunders joins her, and they are married, Miss Denby obviously acting as bridesmaid and one of the witnesses. Now, do they all come home to Maunsby together? I think not. My guess is that the two girls took one route, and Saunders another, and that the three met at Ellwood House. I think Gillian and Sally Denby rang Rhoda Maddison from there—the call that was supposed to be made from Canal Road.

"Miss Denby has to be taken home, and that is done. Saunders still has to keep up the play with Rhoda, and if he has to call her as if he had just reached town from London he has to use a call-box, and not a private 'phone—taking coin-box noises into account. It would be unwise to come into the village, so where is the next nearest call-box to his house, Lancaster? Outside the village, I mean."

"At the junction of Woodstock Lane and the main Maunsby road. Perhaps eight or nine minutes in his car."

"Which would cover the midnight call," said Knollis. "It must have been Saunders' own car Rhoda Maddison saw from the attic, although she accepted the idea that it was a taxi. This gives me a new line on the rifling of Maddison's bureau. All three were interested in Maddison's marriage ban; Saunders and Gillian because they had a marriage arranged, and Rhoda because she thought she was going to marry Saunders sooner or later. We have to look for the stronger motive, which seems to me to be the joint one of Saunders and Gillian."

"They wangled Saunders' entry to the house," murmured Lancaster.

"Yes, the rope proved that. The doors were diametrically opposite, and could have been tied without bringing the radiator into the matter at all. All the slack hung from the handle of Gillian's door, proving she was the last to be tied in her room. What then happened? It seems to me that Gillian tied her aunt in her room, went downstairs to meet her husband—the celluloid still being in place, and afterwards he covered her by roping her door. Up to now the whole thing is obvious."

"It follows," Lancaster said slowly, "but how did you arrive at the idea of the marriage? Where was the initial clue, because I'm blessed if I saw it!"

"You know," Knollis confided, "I'm secretly afraid of this case! It's been all too easy up to now. The presence of the beret and the gloves at Ellwood House started me thinking. Saunders is an ex-army regular, an habitual disciplinarian, and not likely to allow the staff to take liberties in the house. It couldn't have been Rhoda's beret, so I guessed it belonged to Gillian. She must have been so regular and so favoured a visitor to the house that she could fling her belongings down just where she chose.

"Secondly, Saunders told us he was not going to marry Rhoda. Thirdly, he and Gillian had been out of the village at the same time. Fourthly, it was obvious by the way Rhoda couldn't keep her eyes off Gillian's gold chain that it was new—something Rhoda hadn't seen before. Therefore it seemed possible that it had been bought while Gillian was on holiday. It was too expensive a present for a working girl like Sally Denby to buy, and that made me think again. I knew my deduction was correct when I found the crucifix. Women tend to be both sentimental and superstitious, and I think a woman would only remove a crucifix from her neck in order to re-place it with something of still more sentimental value. Up to now the case has been pure textbook stuff!"

"A wedding ring," murmured Lancaster.

"Exactly," said Knollis. "You see, Lancaster, there's seldom smoke without at least a spark of fire, and as soon as I heard of the village gossip about Saunders and Gillian I suspected at least a grain of truth in it. All the village said Saunders and Gillian were attracted to each other, but only Rhoda said Saunders was going to marry *her*."

"That's true," agreed Lancaster. "Now where do we go from here?"

"If Gillian had taken the crucifix from the chain while in the bedroom she would surely have hidden it," mused Knollis. "The fact that it was found in the sitting-room indicates that it was removed during a sentimental and passionate scene with her husband—you're a married man, Lancaster, so I can leave that to your imagination. For some reason or other they now regarded it as safe for Gillian to wear her ring, even if only in her bosom. And while I'll never be able to prove it, I'm prepared to wager that Rhoda had then seen the crucifix which was normally hidden within Gillian's clothes."

"I see," said Lancaster slowly. "She was so engrossed with the business of transferring the ring to the chain that she ignored the crucifix, or forgot it."

"That's what I think," nodded Knollis. "I'm only hoping Rhoda Maddison hadn't spotted it before I got it in my pocket."

"The strip of celluloid," said Lancaster.

"I'm right down to guesswork now," Knollis said with a wry smile. "It was obviously fixed before Maddison's death, and that gives us two lines of investigation. Either Saunders and Gillian had planned for Saunders to enter the inn one night and go through Maddison's papers, or somebody else had planned to get in to murder Maddison, or Saunders and Gillian planned to do both. I don't know the answer to that riddle."

"What about Rhoda Maddison for the major role?"

"Ye—es," Knollis admitted reluctantly, "she had everything needed for it—motive, capability, and opportunity, An unmarried woman of her age is a frustrated woman unless she's found some channel through which to dissipate her energy. She appears to have spent all her time at the inn, with no social activities or outlets. She could have done it, Lancaster. A coldly calculating intellect backed by a strong emotional urge!"

Lancaster said: "Hm!"

"I'm going out to Ellwood House in the morning," said Knollis. "I want you to ring Saunders and ask him if he can spare the time to run into town to see you—you want information about archery. I'll interview his man, Bates, while he's away. I'll be taking a car and a sergeant, so get Saunders to run you back to his home, where I'll be waiting."

Lancaster rang Saunders. "He's coming over at nine, so you'd better tell Mac to run you the long way round if you don't want to meet Saunders."

The sergeant picked up Knollis at the hotel at a quarter to nine the next morning. Alfred Bates was surprised to see them when he answered the door-bell. "The Captain's only just gone into town to see Inspector Lancaster, sir!"

"Must have got our signals crossed," Knollis replied smoothly. "Think we could come in and wait for a few minutes?"

Bates could do no more than ask them to step inside. The morning sun was shining through the open door of the morning-room, lighting the motes of dust playing round the hall-chest, on which lay the beret and gloves.

"I've a question to ask you," said Knollis. "How many people slept in this house on the night Captain Saunders returned from London?"

Bates appeared to be genuinely surprised by the question. "How many, sir? Why, only the Captain and me. The two girls are off."

Knollis half-closed an eye. "Sure of that? The Captain didn't perhaps slip down and let someone in after you retired to your own quarters?"

Bates was indignant. "The Captain's a good-living gentleman, sir!"

"At what time did the two young ladies come?" asked Knollis.

"Er—well, it was lateish," said Bates, "but they all had a drink together, and then the Captain ran them back to town."

"He brought them, of course!"

"Well, yes."

"And you're sure Miss Gillian Maddison did not return with him?"

Bates sniffed. "I was waiting at the gates when he came back, so's I could shut them for the night, and unless she was hiding in the back, or hanging on the back axle . . ."

"You think I'm making assertions against Captain Saunders and Miss Maddison, Bates?"

"Well, it does sound a bit like it, sir, if you don't mind me saying so."

"I don't," said Knollis. "Suppose I told you that Captain Saunders and Miss Maddison are married?"

Bates studied the carpet for a moment, and then looked up. "Oh, so you know, sir!"

"You knew?"

"I went over as witness, but the Captain swore me to secrecy—on account of the other Miss Maddison, you see."

"Good enough," said Knollis. "Now we can get back to the original question. Did Mrs. Saunders spend the night here with her husband?"

"The answer's still the same, sir. She didn't. He ran her back to town with her friend, and came back alone."

"Damn!" said Knollis, biting his lip viciously.

He looked hard at Bates. "You were around all the time the girls were here?"

"I was, sir. Being a witness, I was one of the little party as you might say."

"Miss Denby being the second witness?"

"Er—yes."

"Did Miss Denby make a 'phone call while she was here?"

"No, sir, and I'll swear to that."

"At what time did Captain Saunders get back from Maunsby?"

"Oh, ten to a quarter past twelve, sir."

"I see," said Knollis. "By the way, has Captain Saunders any business interests, or is he completely independent?"

"He's independent sir. His father left him a large sum of money."

"At what time does he rise, Bates?"

"I take his cup of tea at seven, and he takes breakfast at half-past."

"He never breaks the rule?"

"I can't remember him doing so, sir?"

"Not even the morning after he returned from—shall we say London?"

"Not even then, sir," Bates persisted.

Knollis sighed. "We'll look round the garden while we're waiting for him."

Lancaster eventually arrived with Captain Saunders, and after somewhat weak excuses had been made for the overlapping interviews, Knollis took his colleague back to the cellar of the Fox.

The switch for the lamp lighting the stairs was in the bar, while a bank of three switches on the cellar wall served the two lights in the main cellar and the single one in the wine cellar. There, in the main cellar, the shaded lamp nearer the target cupboard had been drawn up to the ceiling by a length of string, so that the light was focussed on the target. Knollis switched on this light and went to stand before the target, while Lancaster watched him from a point half-way along the cellar.

"Move back towards the steps," said Knollis. "Hm! From here I'm so blinded by the light that I can't tell whether you're still here or not. That's interesting in itself."

"Which means that Maddison's assailant could surprise him providing he or she moved silently?"

Knollis nodded, and turned to examine the target, riddled with small round holes as if it had been used for miniature-bore rifle practice.

"Also interesting!" he commented. "Back in a few minutes."

He left Lancaster standing aimlessly in the cellar while he ran lightly to the ground floor.

"I've asked Saunders to come down," he explained when he returned. "There's a point we almost missed."

He led Lancaster along to the target, and pointed to it. "Sort the thing out for yourself!"

"Thanks," said Lancaster.

Lancaster turned from the target with a shrug, and they chatted about other aspects of the case for some ten minutes, when a voice called "Stick 'em up!" and Lancaster span round to see Captain Saunders standing under the second lamp, a drawn bow in his hands.

"Thanks!" said Knollis. "We didn't hear a sound."

Saunders let down the bow and un-nocked the arrow. "I'll put my shoes on now," he said. "I came down with them in my hand, and this floor is not one of Major Oliver's fire-walking causeways by any manner of means."

"Who is Major Oliver?" asked Knollis.

"Old boy who lives on Woodstock Lane. Boring old so-and-so, too. He spent a lot of time in India and claims to be a Yogi. He'd like to marry Rhoda if she'd have him."

He slipped his feet into his shoes and tied the laces. "And the next, Inspector?"

"You've brought a hunting arrow?"

"I've brought both sets, the spear-heads and the bodkins."

"I'd like you to shoot one of each at the target," said Knollis, "aiming at the bull's-eye."

"The gold," corrected Saunders.

"Stand as far back as is practicable without hindering your shooting."

Captain Saunders waved them back. "Better come to my end of the cellar. I haven't done much shooting with these arrows, and being differently balanced they might go wild." He pulled a leather shooting tab over the first and third fingers of his right hand, and nocked the arrow on the string of his bow. He look calculatingly at the height of the ceiling from the floor, and drew the bow, the string being drawn hard into his chin. There was a twang, and the arrow buried itself deeply in the target. He nocked the second arrow, drew, released, and the arrow sped along the cellar.

Saunders grunted. "Lousy shooting! The bodkin is too high—it would be about in the blue at one o'clock, and the spear-head too low—white at six o'clock."

"All of which is Greek to us," said Lancaster.

Saunders laid his bow aside and plunged his hands in his jacket pockets. "Cue for a short lecture," he grinned. "The standard target is four feet wide, and the gold—or bull as you call it—is just over nine inches wide. The rings round it are red, blue, black, and white, in that order—outwards. The gold counts nine, and the others consecutively seven, five, three and one."

"I'm interested in the bodkin one you shot," said Knollis. "Look here, and you'll see what I mean."

He turned the right door of the cupboard on its hinges and indicated a chalked ring. "You see, Captain Saunders, the arrow that missed Maddison was a bodkin-pointed one, and landed here. The one that hit him landed through his heart. Now Lancaster's the tallest of us, and you'll see that if he stands in front of the target the position of the spear-head is approximately level with his heart. Interesting, isn't it?"

Saunders scraped the floor with the toe of his shoe. "I'm not at all sure what you're getting at, but the bodkin, while heavy, flies truer to aim than the spear-head. Apart from being streamlined with the shaft of the arrow it's also fluted—the pile, or business end, I mean. I'm not trying to confuse you with technical terms. The spear-head is an unbalanced effort, naturally, and far more nose-heavy . . ."

He sought for words for a few seconds. "You see, at the one end of the arrow you have three feathers, spaced equidistantly. At the pile you have, in effect, two projections—the wings of the spear . . ."

"I see what you mean," Knollis nodded. "Now I'd like you to take the arrows from the target."

Saunders placed the first and second fingers of his left hand fork-wise round each arrow in turn, pressed on the target, and withdrew the arrows with his right hand. Knollis examined the target closely and sighed.

"That settles that, Lancaster. Have the whole cupboard removed to headquarters as soon as possible. It is Exhibit Number One in the case Rex versus An Unknown. Now, Captain Saunders, can you give us the address of the bow-maker at Brookdale—isn't Cowan his name?"

Saunders sought for his wallet. "I'll give you his card; Huntsman Archery Equipment. His house is just off the market square. You'll like him. Red-haired fellow who breeds posh cats. Professionally, he's an electrical engineer, and makes archery tackle on the side. Making a go of it, too, mainly because his stuff is good."

Knollis led him to the ground floor with his equipment. "Thanks for everything. Staying here?"

"I'll scrounge a coffee in the kitchen," said Saunders, "and try to sense the atmosphere, which I think will be somewhat strained."

* * *

Cowan was as interested in Knollis and Lancaster as they were in him. He eyed them happily. "I always wanted to meet a detective or so, but never thought it would be in the way of business. What can I do for you—as if I couldn't guess!"

"Recognise this?" asked Knollis, producing Maddison's bow, for which they had called on the way.

Cowan nodded. "One of mine. I made it for Maddison at the Fox at Teverby, the fellow who's been murdered."

"Make anything else for him?"

"A set of seven twenty-eight inch arrows."

"Can you describe them?"

"Oh yes. Normal target arrows—that's like these with the bullet noses. They were anodised, wood-yellow, with red shaft feathers and green cock feathers, and the cresting—that's these decorative rings—was red, blue, and gold."

Lancaster raised his eyebrows and glanced at Knollis, who did not appear to be surprised by the information.

"You keep records of sales?"

"Yes."

"You've made tackle for most of the Teverby Bowmen?"

"Nearly all of them, yes."

"You can provide particulars of tackle sold to the Misses Maddison?"

Cowan reached a ledger from a shelf. He bent over the table and wrapped his legs together. "Miss Rhoda Maddison had a five-feet-six bow of lemonwood backed with yew, and a dozen and a half arrows, six made of Port Orford cedar, and the rest metal, all twenty-seven inchers—she has longish arms for a woman.

"Miss Gillian had a five-feet-three bow of osage orange. I didn't want her to have it because it was frankly an experimental effort, but she insisted it was just what she wanted, so there you are. She had a dozen twenty-five inch metal arrows. I also fitted them with tabs and bracers."

"And they are—what?" asked Knollis.

"The bracer is the leather shield one wears on the left forearm to prevent bruising by the string when it is released. The tab is a small pad of leather with two finger-holes in it; that is to prevent the string cutting the fingers as the bow is drawn."

Knollis rubbed his chin thoughtfully. "Can you spare the time to run back into Maunsby with us? I'd rather like you to look at something. An expert opinion would be valuable just now."

"Get going," said Cowan, "and I'll follow in my van. Going to the police station?"

"We are," said Knollis.

The cupboard from the cellar of the Fox was being carried into the building as they arrived. Lancaster had it taken through to the main C.I.D. office and reared against the wall. Knollis opened the doors, revealing the improvised target.

"Now, Mr. Cowan, I'd like you to inspect this target and say how many spear-headed or bodkin-pointed arrows have been shot into it. Take your time. There's no hurry."

He handed round his cigarettes and lighter, and went to the window to look down into the busy courtyard. Lancaster watched him curiously. He was the weirdest bird he had met in nineteen years of police experience. He observed, and thought, and kept his ideas to himself until they were proved. It might be good investigation, but it was not good teamwork, and in Lancaster's opinion it was a method of riding high for a mighty fall; detection in these days relied on the combined efforts of detectives of all ranks. However, those who lived would see!

Cowan turned from the target. "I won't be dogmatic, but I'll say one of each has been shot into it, and no more. And one bodkin-pointed has been shot into the outside of the right-hand door."

"Can you show us where they landed?" asked Knollis.

"Easy! The bodkin in the blue at half-past twelve to one o'clock. The spear-head in the white at six o'clock."

Knollis thanked him, and got rid of him before smiling slyly at Lancaster.

"Maddison did not take the two arrows from the shelf behind the bar, Lancaster. That leaves us with Saunders, Rhoda Maddison, and Gillian Maddison—unless there's an unknown in the case, which I doubt."

"Pardon my obtuse mind," Lancaster murmured somewhat sarcastically, "but how the devil did you arrive at those conclusions?"

"Cowan told us that Maddison bought a set of arrows from him?"

"Why, yes."

"And that only two hunting arrows have been shot into this home-made target?"

"That's obvious by the different shapes of hole they've made."

"Then Maddison couldn't have been practising with them, could he?"

"No—o," Lancaster admitted reluctantly.

Knollis brought his fingers into play once more as he ticked off his facts. "So that means that Maddison must have been using the arrows bought from Cowan. It means that someone else stole the arrows from the bar. It means that someone not only left the two hunting arrows on the scene with the object of making it appear that he was using them, and them only, and was the person who filched them, but also removed Maddison's set of normal arrows to enhance the intended effect."

"Yes," Lancaster said again.

Knollis narrowed his eyes until they were mere slits.

"Maddison's arrows are twenty-eight inches long. Both Saunders and Rhoda Maddison use twenty-seven inch arrows. Gillian uses twenty-five inch arrows . . ."

"Making what?"

Knollis gave a wry smile. "That's the point, isn't it? The first arrow shot at Maddison—we'll assume the bad miss was the first—went high. The second one took him through the heart."

"All that should add up to something," said Lancaster.

"It does, Lancaster! It does! The arrows that killed Maddison were twenty-seven inches long. Well, we've the beginnings of the case, and now we've got the end, and all we need is the middle. There's a deal of hard work ahead of us!"

Lancaster leaned against the table, pop-eyed, and waited, but Knollis made no attempt to qualify his statement. Instead he looked up at the wall-clock and said: "Nearly twelve. A little early for lunch, but I think we should take it now, and see what a long afternoon brings forth. You agree?"

Chapter VIII
THE EVIDENCE OF SAUNDERS

KNOLLIS LUNCHED ALONE at his hotel, barely conscious that he was eating as he pondered on the Maddison case. Up to now, as he had warned Lancaster, it had been far too easy. Information had tumbled into his lap instead of having to be sought out and dragged in by the tail like a reluctant cat. That meant that the evidence supplied by the witnesses to date, and so readily, was a *façade* behind which existed another story.

Working backwards from Maddison's death, the evidence came to an abrupt halt at the point where Saunders had got involved in an argument regarding the efficiency of his hunting arrows, and it was over this that he puzzled as he automatically worked his way through an excellent lunch.

"You see, Lancaster," he said when he got back to police head-quarters, "I'm wondering if it was planned for Saunders to take his arrows to the Fox to be stolen. I'm no believer in coincidence, although I am prepared to believe in accident—meaning that someone saw an opportunity and snatched it. Suppose we have another talk to Saunders, and then call on this Major Oliver?"

"You've made up your mind to that course?" Lancaster asked in a deceptively innocent tone.

"Yes, I have," replied Knollis.

"Then why ask me?" demanded Lancaster irascibly. "The car's waiting in the street, so let's go."

Captain Saunders met them at his door with a twisted smile. "I'll offer you digs any time at all," he said. "What's the trouble this time?"

"Another necessary chat," said Knollis. "Shall we stroll in the garden? It's too nice a day to be indoors."

Saunders shrugged and joined them in a stroll across the lawns to the summerhouse behind the shrubbery.

"I'm puzzled about the arrows," explained Knollis. "Can you remember how the argument started—the conversation that ended in you taking the arrows to the inn?"

"Well, yes," Saunders said slowly. "It was just one of those discussions that turn up in smoke-rooms. Major Oliver was on his favourite hobby-horse, the cult of Yoga, and I intentionally upset him, and then made the suggestion that he should teach me something of eastern philosophy and in return I'd teach him to shoot. He went on to ridicule my archery, and compared my tackle with native stuff he's seen in Mongolia, saying a Mongol bow would kill a yak at a hundred yards or some such distance. I told him about the draw-weight or strength of modern bows and said I'd take my hunting arrows down for him to look at. If that didn't satisfy him I'd demonstrate them on the archery field."

"I see," said Knollis. "Can you remember who else was in the room?"

Saunders narrowed his eyes in the Knollis manner as he attempted to visualise the room.

"Maddison was leaning over the half-door. Williams from the farm, was in the farm corner, and Doughty, the chemist from the next village, was sitting directly opposite me. I'm sure there was no one else present at the time."

"Neither of the Misses Maddison were present?" Saunders shook his head.

"Now for the night when the arrows were stolen. Who was in the room that night?"

"Only myself, Oliver, Maddison, and Williams. Then the coach party came in and spread itself round the house. The arrows were then in the bar, on the shelf under the spirit bottles."

"And the ladies?"

"Rhoda was serving behind the bar. Gillian came in after the coach party arrived, to help with the unexpected rush of trade."

"Where were the two ladies while the rush was on?"

"Gillian took over our room. Maddison and Rhoda were sharing the long bar, and Roberts was handling the tap-room pumps at the far end, beyond the partition. After the Roberts' incident, Maddison took the tap-room, and Rhoda had the long bar to herself, serving the orders collected by Rose Cromwell and the other girl."

"That's all perfectly clear," said Knollis. "Was Miss Gillian in the smoke-room all the time?"

"Yes, there's no doubt about that."

"So that Miss Rhoda was virtually alone in the long bar, and the arrows were on the shelf behind her?"

"Yes, I'm afraid that is a fact," Saunders said reluctantly.

"You had your car there—in the park?"

"Oh yes."

"Major Oliver has a car?"

"Yes, a somewhat disreputable two-seater."

"That was in the park?"

"No—o, I seem to remember he left it against the kerb."

"The chemist, Doughty; he had a car there?"

"Ye—es, I think that was parked behind Oliver's, on the street."

"I don't know Major Oliver," said Knollis, "so cannot gauge his manner. Was it provocative, or was he leg-pulling when inferring that your archery tackle was not all it might be?"

"Provocative," smiled Saunders. "He's a dogmatic and bigoted old josser who gets up my back and into my hair. I dodge him whenever possible."

"Know anything about him? Where he comes from, and how long he's lived in Teverby?"

"He comes from somewhere below London, and has been here since a few months after the end of the war. More than that I can't say, except that he's a bachelor and badly wants to marry Rhoda."

"There's no impediment now, is there?" Knollis said softly.

Saunders glanced at him, and shrugged. "Maddison's gone, of course."

"Hasn't Bates recounted my interview with him this morning?" asked Knollis.

"I didn't know you had interviewed him," replied Saunders. "He's said nothing to me. I wouldn't expect him to do so, anyway. He keeps other people's confidences as he keeps mine."

"You aren't interested in what I asked him?"

"One shouldn't be interested in other people's business," retorted Saunders. He added: "Unless one is engaged on an official investigation, as you are."

"This trip to London," said Knollis.

"What about it?"

Knollis took out his cigarette case and offered it to Saunders and Lancaster. Saunders supplied the lighter.

"Suppose we clear the decks," said Knollis. "We know you got yourselves married last week—you and Miss Gillian."

Saunders lowered an eyelid. "Bates surely didn't let you pump that from him!"

"Bates is an admirable confidant," smiled Knollis. "He wouldn't even admit that the sun came up on Tuesday. Your confidence in him is deserved. No, we found out in our own peculiar ways—first a clue, and then a theory, and then the proof."

Saunders studied the lighted end of his cigarette and said: "Hm!"

"Your wife *is* wearing her wedding ring on that gold chain round her neck?" Knollis asked casually.

Saunders nodded. "Yes, you're correct."

There was a moment's silence, and then he asked: "I'd like to know how you got at us."

"You were too careless in the emotional excitement of the moment," explained Knollis. "You threw the crucifix on the settee. I rescued it before Miss Rhoda saw it—I think. Here it is if you'd like to return it to your wife. She may treasure it."

Saunders stared at the crucifix lying in his hand. He appeared to be completely at a loss for something to say, and finally thanked Knollis weakly.

"You did the swop in the middle of the night, of course," suggested Knollis.

"Oh?" murmured Saunders.

"Miss Gillian, your wife I should say, roped her aunt's door and went down to meet you. On the completion of the business you roped her door, and let yourself out. That is the truth, isn't it, Captain Saunders?"

"Yes," said Saunders.

"We now get to two interesting points," went on Knollis conversationally. "When did you fix the celluloid strip over the latchbox, and what have you done with Maddison's private papers?"

Saunders blinked, shook his head, and came to life again. "I didn't fit the celluloid, and neither did Gillian, believe it or not. And Maddison's bureau was already rifled when Gillian and I got to it. So far as the strip was concerned, well, Gillian found a small screwdriver and I removed it before I left—thinking about her safety. It's here," he said, opening his wallet. "I'll give it to you in exchange for the crucifix—I was worrying about that in case Rhoda found it and put two and two together."

"Nice of you," Knollis said placidly. "Now why did you choose that particular night to effect the exchange? It rather interests me."

"It was safe," replied Saunders. "Rhoda had searched Gillian's room after she was supposed to be asleep, and found the crucifix attached to the chain. That should have satisfied any doubts she might have had—you see, the chain was bought in Eastness, and Rhoda hadn't seen it before."

"She surely took a great risk," said Knollis as an idea presented itself to him. "Miss Rhoda hadn't doped her by any chance? Or had she? Or attempted to dope her?"

Saunders stuck the cigarette in the corner of his mouth and plunged his hands deep into his jacket pockets. "Look here, Inspector, how much do you know?"

"The extent of one's knowledge is always comparative," Knollis murmured non-committally. "On any given subject I might know less than Inspector Lancaster and more than you, or vice versa. I repeat; why did your wife and yourself choose that particular night for a passionate tryst and a delving into Maddison's papers?"

"Oh well," sighed Saunders. "Let's sit down to it, shall we?"

He walked into the summer-house and drew three wicker chairs forward from the wall.

"The whole thing went like this. Gillian rang me rather late and asked me to call her aunt in a few minutes' time, and keep her occupied for about four or five minutes. She also told me to let myself into the house after midnight. I did both, and when I got to the inn she was waiting for me in the lobby. She then told me the story. Just before ringing she'd caught her aunt poking about in the bureau, and at the same time milk was warming in the kitchen for their nightcaps. She got rid of her aunt, opened the secret drawer, and found a box of pheno-barbitone tablets. Her aunt had left the room with one hand tightly clenched, and that gave Gillian the idea that Rhoda might possibly want her to sleep soundly for some reason or other. Hence the 'phone call to me. I was to keep Rhoda engaged on the line while Gillian was switching the drinks—and adding three more tablets to Rhoda's milk just to make sure."

"You said she'd been doped," murmured Lancaster.

"Go on," said Knollis as Saunders paused.

"Gillian went to bed first, and Maddison's papers were all neatly filed in the bureau at that time, so we've assumed that Rhoda took them before going into Gillian's room."

He gave a wry grin. "If we'd have thought that one out in time I'd have left the strip on the door so that I could have got into the house again."

"You're honest, anyway," said Knollis. "You won't object to having your finger-prints taken, will you? Only two people should have handled this strip. Once we've sorted out yours we can look for the owner of whatever prints are left."

"That's all right," said Saunders. "I've nothing to fear. You can have them in technicolour for all I care. By the way, Rhoda doesn't know about our marriage, does she?"

"We haven't told her, and there's no reason why we should," replied Knollis. "That's your own business. One thing I would like from you is a frank account of your movements on the evening and night when you returned from—er—London."

"Nothing to it," shrugged Saunders. "I didn't want to be seen coming home with Gillian, so I took an earlier train and a roundabout route so that it would appear that I had come from

London if anyone noticed me at Maunsby. I landed there shortly before Gillian and brought her and her friend back here for a celebratory drink, and then ran them back to town."

"Making a 'phone call to Miss Rhoda Maddison from where?"

Saunders smiled. "The call box at the bottom of Woodstock Lane."

"A friend posted the letters for you?"

"Oh yes, I sent them three days before with full instructions."

"That clears everything up beautifully," smiled Knollis. Quickly he asked: "Your wife returned here to sleep with you?"

"No," said Saunders, shaking his head. "We thought it wiser for her to stay with Miss Denby. We had Rhoda to think about you know, and news travels mysteriously in a village like this! And Michael, of course! We didn't know he would be dead by morning."

"When did you first learn about the celluloid strip?"

"After Inspector Lancaster discovered it—and that is the truth."

"Why has it been assumed that there was something of interest to be found among Maddison's papers, Captain Saunders."

Saunders scratched his head. "We—ell, we didn't know whether there was or not, but Maddison's attitude was so peculiar! Why should he put bans on the two girls marrying? What was he going to lose if they did marry? How could he possibly benefit if they didn't? How else could our minds work? You do see the point!"

"You've no clue to the answers?" asked Knollis.

"Not a single one," sighed Saunders. "The whole thing is incomprehensible. We're whacked with it! And we can't very well delve farther now you fellows are on the case," he said wryly.

"Don't forget that, either!" warned Knollis. "Where did Maddison come from?"

"He was living in a quiet lane somewhere outside Woking," said Saunders. "Rhoda's always been puzzled about two things; why Maddison parked them there in the first place, and why he came to Teverby. And there's a point puzzling me, one I haven't mentioned to a soul until now—how did he, without any previous experience, get the tenancy of a village inn? Had you thought about that?"

"I've had no need to think about it," confessed Knollis, "but I will do. Well, we'd better leave you. Thanks for all your help, Captain Saunders. Grateful, aren't we, Lancaster?"

They drove to Woodstock House. Major Oliver boomed a welcome and invited them indoors. "Don't drink before sundown, myself, but if you fellows should like a drink . . ."

"We're on duty, thanks," said Knollis.

They followed him through an entrance hall decorated with souvenirs of his years in the East to a well-stocked library.

"We don't really know whether you can help us or not," said Knollis when they were seated, "but we wonder if you saw or heard anything suspicious on the night of Maddison's death—that is, the few hours previous to it."

"Queer you should ask that," said the major. "I was debating with myself whether to come and see you or not. There were too many cars dashing about. Made me think something was happening. Round about half-past eleven a car dashed past from Maunsby. Just before midnight a car dashed back again. Quarter past the hour, and a car came from Maunsby. Looked like the same car—dunno for sure. Looked like Saunders'—not certain, y'know! That wasn't all, of course!"

"Wasn't it?" asked Knollis quietly.

"Not by any manner of means, sir! It was a most oppressive night, and I couldn't sleep. Different heat to what you get out East, of course. It's the humidity, not the heat, that gets you down. Out there, of course, with temperatures of a hundred and—"

"What did you see, Major Oliver?" Knollis interrupted.

"Eh? Oh yes! Well, it was oppressive, so I walked to the drive gates and stood there admiring the stars. Heard a sound, and saw a fellow pedalling up the lane on a bike without lights. There's a field gate just below, as you may have noticed. He propped the bike there, climbed the gate, and set off across the fields towards Saunders' place. No doubt where he was going—making a beeline for it. I thought I recognised him, but wasn't sure, so I went down the lane and hid behind a tree—child's play to me, of course! By the way, I nearly forgot! I had a look at the bike. It was a lady's, with a panel in the lid of the tool-bag, only the celluloid was missing—"

"The name-card?" Knollis interrupted quickly. "Was that in evidence?"

Major Oliver nodded. "Yes, the bike was Miss Maddison's!"

"Miss Gillian's?"

"Miss Rhoda's, sir."

"Mm!" said Knollis.

"Mysterious business, sir," boomed the major. "I couldn't get the hang of it at all, so parked myself behind the tree and waited. Must have been another quarter of an hour before he came back, mounted the bike, and rode off down the lane."

"And it was . . . ?"

"Maddison, sir."

"The time was then . . ."

"Twenty to one when I got back to the house. First thing I did was look at the clock."

Knollis stared at the wall. The 'phone call to Rhoda Maddison came at a few minutes after midnight, and she then went to bed, leaving Maddison "doing his accounts." Saunders would be back home from Maunsby shortly after a quarter past twelve, and Maddison was, if Oliver's times were correct, in the lane at twenty past twelve. It all added up to something—but what?

"What I really came to ask you about," he said, "was the evening when Captain Saunders' arrows vanished from the bar of the inn. You were there at the time?"

"Peculiar business," murmured Major Oliver. "I'll swear Saunders never went near the serving-hatch, so it was no leg-pull. He'd no need to go, because Miss Gillian was waiting on us in the smoke-room. Can't see anyone for it but Maddison himself."

"How did the arrows come to be there at all, Major Oliver?" asked Knollis.

"Result of an argument, Inspector. The result of an argument. Saunders was decrying the Mongolian bows I'd been telling him about, and offered to do anything the Mongols could do. He brought the arrows to show me, and I must admit I was impressed. Some day I must go down and try the stuff out, just to satisfy myself. These things of Saunders' are nice-looking and all that, but I still doubt if they'd come up to the sinew-backed bows the Mongols use."

"You've—er—used the Mongolian bows?" Knollis asked innocently.

"Oh yes, sir! Definitely lose prestige if you don't prove yourself capable with native weapons. Definitely lose face. Oh yes! Damn-awful things to brace and draw, and they've a kick like a mule if you don't release properly. The string just whips down the forearm and tears into flesh and muscle like a butcher's knife."

"Er—could I dare to ask a very delicate question, Major?" Knollis asked with a good show of embarrassment.

The major waved expansively. "Ask what you like, sir! I'm not bound to give you an answer, am I?"

Knollis coughed behind his hand. "Er—well, Major Oliver, do you happen to be interested in either of the Misses Maddison?"

"Interested?" boomed the major. "Dammit, man, I'm going to *marry* Miss Rhoda, and don't give a hang who knows it!"

"Then she has—er—accepted you?"

Major Oliver looked down at his feet, and snorted. "No, she hasn't. Matter of fact she's turned me down three times, but I'll keep going! Things may be different now Maddison's out of the way."

"She told you he had certain objections?"

"Yes, the woman's straightforward—that's what I like about her. I didn't know the real trouble until this morning, of course, when I got talking to her at the inn."

Knollis hardly dared to move, and hoped Lancaster would not butt in with a destructive remark.

Major Oliver cocked an eyebrow. "When you meet a decent woman you appreciate her," he said. "She wouldn't accept me now, not until her brother's death is cleared up, but when it is settled she'll be in a position to say yes. Couldn't do it before, you know!"

"No?" murmured Knollis.

"Wouldn't come to me as a pauper without a dowry because it would have looked as if she was marrying for security only, and not for her—herrum!—love for me."

"And the way will be free now?" Knollis asked in the gentlest of tones.

"Well," Major Oliver demanded in a loud voice, "who is left to stop her getting at her own money? And it has been her own money all the time. Trouble was that Maddison, the cad, never let her see what she was signing twice a year!"

"I see," said Knollis.

CHAPTER IX
THE PROGRESS OF GILLIAN

KNOLLIS WAS WORRIED about Major Oliver's evidence. It wasn't that he disbelieved it, but he suspected Rhoda Maddison of having told a second-rate story to the infatuated and credulous major—with a purpose. She was in the middle thirties, a shrewd woman who knew one side of a pound note from the other, and it was difficult to believe she had allowed her brother to keep her in ignorance regarding any money to which she might have been entitled.

He discussed the matter thoroughly with Lancaster, to the latter's surprise, for by now he had become reconciled to acting as Knollis's guide and being told nothing. Knollis then rang Captain Saunders, asking if it would be possible to bring his wife into town without Rhoda Maddison knowing their destination. Saunders thought that could be arranged, and half an hour later came into the office with Gillian on his arm, Gillian still very much the radiant bride in spite of her uncle's tragic and mysterious death. She was neatly dressed in a lightweight grey costume, and did not wear a hat, so that her auburn curls encircled her face like a halo.

"You managed it then," said Knollis.

Saunders gave the characteristic shrug Knollis now knew so well. "It doesn't matter any longer. Rhoda's found out we're married. There's been something of a row at the Fox this afternoon, hasn't there, darling."

"Calling it a row is putting it mildly," said Gillian seriously. "I thought she was going to attack me!"

"How did she find out?"

Gillian grimaced. "My own fault. I was either too careless or too trusting. I hid the marriage certificate under the paper lining in one of my drawers. I, was out all morning, shopping for the funeral, and she went poking round my bedroom. Nothing was said until half-past three this afternoon when the inn was closed and the girls had gone home. Then she came stalking into my room, waving the certificate, and with all hell in her eyes. She called me everything she could think of—and some of the things she thought of weren't nice. I didn't know Aunt Rhoda had a mind like that!"

"And when was this?" Knollis asked curiously.

"Shortly before tea."

Knollis, sitting bolt upright in his chair, traced a curlicue on his note pad with his pen. "Mm! She must have had very early suspicions!"

"Why do you say that?" asked Saunders.

"We can skip that," replied Knollis. "Was your uncle a rich man, Mrs. Saunders?"

"Rich? I wouldn't say that. He was making a good living at the Fox, but nothing to go wild about."

"Was your father a wealthy man?"

"He was pretty well off, but not wealthy. He had some property in the north London district, but Michael told me most of it went west in the blitz."

"Your parents were killed in a raid, were they not?"

"Yes, and my younger sister. That was early in forty-five."

"You would then be how old, Mrs. Saunders?"

"Nearly fifteen. I was at a school in Buckinghamshire."

Knollis made some rapid calculations. "Nearly fifteen, you say. On what date does your birthday fall?"

"The twenty-ninth of September."

"On that date this year you will be twenty-one?" Knollis asked, squinting up from his notes.

"Naturally, Inspector."

"Your uncle's guardianship would have come to an end on that day?"

"Yes."

"Here's a point," said Knollis. "Was there, in the deed of guardianship, any provision made for the circumstances that would arise in the event of your uncle dying before yourself?"

Gillian looked helplessly at her husband.

"I—I don't know. I hadn't thought about it. I was only young at the time, and I really didn't know what was being arranged, other than that Michael was to take care of me."

"Your uncle was on active service then?"

"Yes, he was brought home from Germany to see about me."

"Germany?"

"Well, somewhere on the Continent. I said Germany because that's where he was when he was released from the army."

"He went back, of course?"

"Oh yes!"

"Then what happened to you? Where did you stay? Who looked after you? Where did you work, if anywhere?"

Saunders interposed. "Is all this necessary, Inspector Knollis?"

Knollis extended his hands, palms upwards. "Frankly, Captain Saunders, I don't know, but I'd like the answers."

"An old friend of my mother's took me in. I was living with her at Blackheath until about two months after Michael took the cottage outside Woking. Meanwhile I studied at the Polytechnic and then got a job with Smedley's, the wholesale wine and spirit people. I kept that up to coming to Teverby, and having experience I'd no difficulty in getting another job with my present firm."

"To which she isn't going back," said Saunders fondly.

"I'm interested in the Woking period," Knollis said quietly, as if to himself. "Mrs. Saunders, what was life like with your uncle and aunt?"

"A bit like living in a nunnery," she answered readily. "Michael spent a lot of time away from home, and when he was at home he didn't seem to approve of me going out again once I'd got home from the office. Aunt Rhoda—well, she was just the usual nonentity when Michael was about. She was pleasant, silent, and obedient! I often wondered what she was thinking!"

"Who were the lawyers who arranged his guardianship?" asked Knollis.

"My father's old lawyers, Spears and Bennison of Lincoln's Inn Fields."

"Why didn't you two wait until September before getting married?"

Saunders looked at his wife, and coughed. She looked back at him, and blushed. "We—we wanted to get married!" said Gillian boldly.

"Not considering the trouble which your uncle might have caused?"

"What trouble could he have caused?" demanded Gillian. "Once we were married, we were married!"

"He might have had your marriage annulled," said Knollis, adding to his curlicues.

Gillian came forward on her chair. "He—could he have done that?"

Knollis nodded.

Gillian said: "Oh!"

"Suppose it turns out that your aunt takes over the guardianship until September, Mrs. Saunders? Your husband has told us of the—er—difficulties that have arisen between you."

It was Captain Saunders who replied. "Oh lord!" he exclaimed. "I hadn't thought about that!"

Gillian looked from Knollis to Lancaster, and from Lancaster to her husband with a worried frown. "You mean that Aunt Rhoda could still have my marriage annulled?"

"It would hardly be worth while now," said Knollis, "but she could institute the necessary proceedings if she was your guardian."

Gillian tossed her head so that the auburn curls danced on her slim shoulders. "She's had it! As for Michael, why should he have been so unreasonable? Why did he object? How could my marriage concern him?"

"I wonder," said Knollis, throwing his pen across the table. He pushed his chair back on its two rear legs, and plaited his fingers behind his head. "That's what I'm trying to find out, Mrs. Saunders. It might equally affect your aunt."

"If any court annulled our marriage I'd still live with Harry and defy them all!" snapped Gillian.

"Winding up in gaol for contempt of court," smiled Knollis. "Don't take it for granted, and don't jump streams until you get to them, Mrs. Saunders. You're still young and impetuous, if you don't mind me saying so. We don't know that your aunt does take you over, and we don't know that she wants to have your marriage annulled, so we can leave those two points and go on to something else."

Saunders had been silent throughout most of the interview, watching his wife and Knollis as they threw question and answer across the wide leather-topped table. Now he leaned forward, his hands on his knees. "I think I'm getting into your mind at least, Inspector. I shall take my wife home with me now the cat is out of the bag. She can help Rhoda at the Fox, but I'm staying on the premises whenever she's there!"

"That might be wise," nodded Knollis.

A sudden alarm showed in Gillian's blue eyes. "You mean she might—you mean it was she who—who . . . !"

"We don't know who it was, Mrs. Saunders, and we don't engage in guessing competitions."

"She *was* in the house with him! There were only the two of them that night!"

"The side door was also unlocked," Knollis pointed out. "We can only assume they were alone in the house. What adequate motive could we possibly attribute to your aunt?"

"She wanted Harry," Gillian said in a low voice, and ran her tongue over her lightly made-up lips.

"So did you," said Knollis. "You got him, too!"

"She didn't know that then, Inspector!"

Knollis let his chair fall back on its four legs, and regained his pen. "Are you sure, Mrs. Saunders? Hasn't it occurred to you that she may have suspected the real reason for your seaside holiday? Didn't she search your room?"

"She only *wondered*," said Gillian lamely.

"We're not too sure," said Knollis.

Saunders frowned. "What do you mean, Inspector?"

"We've been told that Michael Maddison was scouting round your house at half an hour after midnight that night, shortly after you got back from Maunsby. Can you suggest any other reason for his presence there, or shall we assume he was trying to find out whether his niece was or was not in your house, married or unmarried?"

"Maddison, eh?" murmured Saunders uncomfortably. "Well, she wasn't there, so we'll assume he was satisfied that his suspicions were unfounded!"

"But if he mentioned them to his sister . . . ?"

"Why should he do that?" demanded Saunders.

"Knowing how matters stood between you," said Knollis, "he might have been seeking an ally."

"An ally?"

"Listen, Captain Saunders," Knollis said patiently. "A man of Michael Maddison's years and experience and so on doesn't put a ban on a young girl's marriage because of pique or what we call sheer cussedness. He was her uncle, and so we can assume he wasn't in love with her himself—"

"Michael was only capable of loving himself!" Gillian interjected.

"Well, there you are," said Knollis. "There was some sound reason why he didn't want her to marry, and why he didn't want Rhoda, his sister, to marry. You think that one out, Captain Saunders, and come back to me when you've found an answer!"

Knollis pushed his chair back, and rose, walking round the table to escort them to the door. "I take it you went straight to bed when you got home from Maunsby, Captain Saunders?"

"I think so, yes. There was nothing to stay up for, and I'd had a hectic day. Yes, I went straight to bed."

With the office to themselves again Knollis and Lancaster looked at each other for a moment, wryly.

"Where are we now?" asked Lancaster.

"Stuck!" Knollis said shortly. "Either Saunders or Rhoda Maddison could have done the job, but the motives are not adequate. Saunders could have got to the inn and back home without being seen at that time of the morning. Rhoda, of course, was already on the premises."

"The celluloid?"

"We'll never prove it, but it came from her bicycle saddlebag. I don't get that. Saunders wasn't keen on her, let alone passionately in love with her, so she wasn't making it easy for him to get into the house o' nights. In any case, it would have been too risky with Michael on the premises, to which we can add her undoubted virtue. That theory won't hold water!"

"Dunno as you're right," said Lancaster. "She *thought* he was keen, and that was what mattered. I'm not suggesting an affair, but supposing she was fixing things so's he could sneak in and take a look at Maddison's documents? Suppose Saunders fell in with the idea because he was in love with Gillian, who was equally affected by Maddison's ban? Suppose she rigged the door while Maddison was supposed to be in London, intending to tell him as soon as he got back?"

"Well, she certainly didn't tell him when he rang her at midnight!" said Knollis. "Judging by what we've been told Maddison must have been within earshot throughout the conversation. Knowing his attitude toward the three of them we can assume that he made sure of hearing everything that was said by Rhoda."

"Ye—es," muttered Lancaster uncertainly. "That means no one but herself knew the door was rigged for an easy entry."

"Unless someone discovered it by accident. We have to take that into account."

"It could be that," agreed Lancaster. "Someone took advantage of the discovery to walk in and try to rob the place."

"Doesn't make sense," grunted Knollis. "Why go down the cellar and skewer him with an arrow? If such an intruder realised Maddison was in the cellar, all he had to do was close the door quietly and lock it from the outside. He could do all he wanted to do, and still get away before Maddison had managed to raise the heavy trapdoors over the delivery chute."

"You're darned right," snorted Lancaster. "Nothing in the case makes sense, does it? All the way through it looks as if whoever was in the house was after Maddison's blood, and that only. But why!"

Knollis squinted down his long nose. "If Rhoda did the job she took a deuce of a risk—a bigger risk than if the house was full of guests."

"And the Saunders couple?"

"Doesn't make sense, either, Lancaster. They were apparently ignorant of the way in which Maddison could invoke the law, and went about it like a pair of innocents, believing that if and when he found out all they had to do was face up to him, say *So What*, and have him stumped!"

"What about Oliver?" murmured Lancaster. "He seems to have been trotting about the village half of the night."

"There's no future in another theory I held for a time," said Knollis. "I wondered if Rhoda might have done the job with the idea of foisting the guilt on to Gillian, thus getting rid of 'em both at one smack, but Gillian wasn't in the house, and she has a nice alibi, and so that's no solution. I hope to blazes we're not going to be whacked with the case, or I'll blow a fuse!"

"Can you get so worked up?" Lancaster asked curiously.

Knollis flung himself into a chair and put his feet up on the desk. "It has been known. Frustration's the only thing that can shake me. I don't mind difficulties providing I can see where I'm going, but this time I'm in the middle of a maze and can't even see the way out of the first alley! Someone has either been very clever or darned lucky."

"What about Oliver?" Lancaster repeated.

"Oliver? What motive?"

"There's a coincidence worrying me," said Lancaster.

"I don't believe in 'em!" said Knollis. "They appear to present coincidental collision of events only because we can't see the cause or the connecting link."

"That is exactly what I'm getting at," Lancaster said slowly and deliberately. "Hasn't it occurred to you that all three men connected with the case are ex-army types?"

Knollis stared at the ceiling for a moment. "No, it hadn't, Lancaster. I didn't even know Maddison was ex-army—or else I've forgotten it."

"Lieutenant-colonel. Even at that he might have done something shady, you know!"

"As likely to have been drummed out of the girl guides," Knollis snarled impatiently. "Let's be sensible, even if we are stuck! No, the only other line to be followed, so far as I can see, is Saunders' suggestion that we find out how Maddison got the pub without any previous experience behind him. Brewery companies are in business to brew and sell beer, and not to encourage amateurs. I think we should see the brewery people in the morning, Lancaster."

The door opened and one of Lancaster's detective-officers put his head into the room. "There's a man you might like to see, sir. He's a long-distance transport driver who was through Teverby at twenty past six on Monday morning."

Knollis took his feet from the desk. "Let's have him in, Lancaster."

The lorry-driver was shown in, pushing his cap into his pocket. "Couldn't get here before sir, but I thought you might be interested."

"In what?" asked Lancaster. "Here, have a chair."

"I took a load up to Liverpool on Monday, sir. It was loaded up for me on Saturday, you see, and I took it over at six on Monday. I was coming over the top road to Teverby when I caught up with a girl on a bike. I took a dekko at her as I passed, and she seemed to be in a bit of a flap. We were over the rise, and she was pedalling as if she was going for a doctor, with her jaw clenched and she was bent low over the handlebars. Pretty kid she was, too."

"About how old?" asked Knollis.

"Nineteen or twenty I gave her, sir."

"Clothes?"

"A green coat with a green and white dress under it—sort of white dress with a green pattern on it. Her coat was flapping open, you see."

"Hair?"

"Fuzzy and curly, and not quite ginger but going that way. She wasn't wearing a hat."

"What time would this be?" asked Lancaster.

"I make it about twenty past six, sir. I got out of town about five to ten past six, but it's a goodish pull up to the old malt-house on the top of the hill. I didn't think much about it at the time, but when I saw in the papers what time Mr. Maddison was killed, well, I just wondered."

"Glad you did," said Knollis. "Good of you to come in. Have you half an hour to spare?"

The driver glanced at the wall-clock. "I'd like a swallow before I turn in."

"There's a pub just round the corner," said Lancaster; "the Bell. Hop round there, and we'll send for you if we should want you again tonight. That be all right?"

He breathed happily as the door closed. "What a break, Knollis!"

"We needed it," sniffed Knollis.

"Sergeant Luck and Inspector Chance, the best two blokes on the Force!"

"And the most reliable! Send for MacFarlane, please, Lancaster."

The sergeant was given his orders. He was to fetch Mrs. Saunders in for questioning, and shed her husband if at all possible.

"And send for Miss Sally Denby of Canal Street for the same purpose, and don't let the two girls meet," added Lancaster.

"That is an idea!" said Knollis.

"I have 'em at times," Lancaster said quietly.

Sally Denby was the first to arrive, and they wasted no time in questioning her.

"You've told us that Miss Maddison spent the night at your house," said Knollis. "Is that the truth?"

"It is," said the scared girl.

"She went to the office with you in the morning?"

"Yes, sir; she really did."

"At what time do you get up?"

"Half-past seven, sir."

"You are the first member of the family to get out of bed?"

"No, sir. My father goes out early, but I slip down to put the kettle on the gas ring, and light the electric fire."

"You saw your friend then?"

"No, sir. I didn't want to disturb her so early. We didn't have to be at the office until nine o'clock."

"At what time did you see her?"

"About ten to eight."

Sally Denby moistened her lips.

"She was obviously not sleeping in the same room as yourself," said Knollis.

"She had the bed-settee in the front room."

Lancaster grunted as if he had seen the light.

"Your father, Miss Denby," went on Knollis; "at what time does he go to work?"

"He gets up at half-past five, sir. My mother lays his breakfast table the night before. He boils his kettle while he's packing his dinner. He's out of the house by five to six."

"We know all about Miss Maddison being married," said Knollis. "We also know you all went to Ellwood House for a drink late on Sunday night. At what time did you go to bed?"

"Just after half-past twelve, sir."

"And didn't see your friend between that time and ten to eight the next morning?"

"No, sir."

"So you can't really say that your friend was in the house all night?"

Sally Denby hesitated. "Well, no, sir, but why should she go out in the night?"

"Quite so," said Knollis. "A silly idea, isn't it? How do you get to work? By bus, or do you walk it?"

"I bike it if it's a nice day, and take the bus if it's raining."

"And on Monday morning you . . . ?"

"Took the bike, but walked it with Gillian. I came home for lunch on it."

"Mrs. Saunders as we must now call her—she had lunch in town?"

"She goes to a café, sir."

"Your cycle is kept—where?"

"In the shed in the yard."

"It is locked?"

"Until my father takes his bike out."

"When you take your bike into the shed," said Knollis, "do you push it straight in, or turn it round ready for wheeling straight out."

Sally Denby pondered. "Wheel it straight in."

"You didn't notice whether it had been moved or not when you went for it on Monday morning?"

"I don't think it looked any different."

"That will be all," said Knollis, smiling to reassure her. "Thanks for coming. The officer will run you back home."

She was led down the back stairs, and Gillian brought in from the opposite direction.

"Mrs. Saunders," said Knollis as she came cautiously into the room, "I find a few more questions I must ask you. Sorry to be such a nuisance, but you know how it is! Please do sit down . . ."

Gillian perched herself on the front edge of the chair and smoothed her grey skirt over her knees, which it only just covered.

"You stayed with your friend, Miss Denby, on the night you returned from Eastness?"

"I surely told you that, Inspector!"

"You did," said Knollis. "You shared a room with her?"

"Oh no! I had the bed-settee in the sitting-room."

"At what time did you rise?"

Gillian put a finger to her lips. "Let me see. I'm not at all sure, but I should say about something to eight—five or ten minutes to eight."

"You—er—slept well?"

She had recovered her composure now, and gave Knollis a cheeky smile. "Yes—considering."

Lancaster coughed behind his hand.

"You weren't disturbed at all?"

Again the sly smile from Gillian. "There was no one to—disturb me, Inspector."

Knollis tapped his fingers on the edge of the table and avoided Lancaster's eyes.

"These silly questions are all necessary, you know," Knollis said apologetically. "Anyway, that's that, and now I'm wondering if you could help us now you are here?"

"If I can, of course. What do you want me to do?"

"We've a bit of trouble in the other part of the building," said Knollis, jerking his thumb at the wall. "A lorry-driver who was driving his vehicle through Teverby at twenty-past six on Monday morning. He saw a girl cycling over what he calls the top road, and has indeed described her in some detail. We have to find her for various reasons, and I wondered if you'd consent to join an identification parade. You know the idea! We get eight or nine people of the same build, colouring, and so on, and ask the witness to, well, find the lady!"

Gillian's eyes widened. "A lorry driver? An identification parade, Inspector?"

She gave a short and uncertain little laugh. "Well, I mean, suppose he makes a mistake?"

"He won't!" said Lancaster from the far side of the room.

"The girl," said Gillian. "What is she—what is she wanted for?"

"Murder," Knollis said shortly.

Gillian Saunders took her lip between her small white teeth and glanced round the room as if looking for a bolt-hole. Lancaster was standing before the door leading to the back stairs, and Sergeant MacFarlane was leaning against the one through which he had brought her, picking his teeth with a match-stick.

"Then you'll help us, Mrs. Saunders?" Knollis said in a relieved tone.

Gillian jumped from her chair, clutching her gloves and hand-bag to her midriff. "No. No! I couldn't do that without my husband's consent! He wouldn't like me to be mixed up with anything like—like—"

"Murder?" suggested Knollis, following her down the room as she backed away from him.

"Yes," she gulped. "Yes, he wouldn't like that!"

"Quite understandable," said Knollis. "Sergeant MacFarlane, please take Mrs. Saunders home again. I'm afraid we've upset her. Most regrettable!"

Chapter X
THE MYSTERY OF MADDISON

LANCASTER WAS SLEEPING uneasily when the telephone roused him at six next morning. He turned over in bed, reached for the instrument, and listened intently. He swung himself to the edge of the bed. "I'll be down right away," he said.

He chuckled as he dialled Knollis's hotel. It was time the fellow was up; he could help with the worrying.

"Lancaster here," he announced. "Just a call from the office. The Teverby constable has brought in a poacher who says he has something to tell us, but will only come clean to me and the London gentleman. See you down there!"

Police-constable Robinson was smiling broadly when Lancaster met him in the corridor and hustled him to the office.

"What's it all about, Robinson?"

"I've been trying to pick up Wilson for the past three months, sir," said Robinson, "and I got him tonight! He's been working Ell Wood, and slipping me every time. I suddenly realised what he was doing—going through an old culvert and coming out on the other side of the boundary, so I waited at the other end for him and caught him with two purse-nets and half a dozen copper snares. They fetched him in for me, and now he says he must see you and Inspector Knollis."

Knollis hurried into the room, still heavy-eyed with sleep, and Robinson repeated his story.

"Better fetch him in," said Lancaster. He turned to Knollis. "John Henry Wilson is one of our die-hard poachers. He's been down four times now, but can't leave the game alone. It's more a hobby than a profession for him."

Wilson was a ferretty little man with a blue and red checked scarf and large dirty hands. He favoured them with an ingratiating smile, and shuffled toward the desk.

Lancaster clicked his tongue sympathetically. "What was it this time, Wilson? Bad luck, or a mistake on the constable's part? Or weren't you there at all and he picked on the wrong man?"

"I wasn't after anything," Wilson said naively. "I just like being out in the moonlight, that's all!"

"And the snares and nets?"

Wilson squirmed and gave a greasy smile. "I found them in the wood, sir! I'd just picked them up when Mr. Robinson came along—and there I was with them in my hands! What could I say?"

"You'll have to learn a new technique," said Lancaster. "You know, learn to charm them out of their burrows, and then you won't be caught in suspicious circumstances. Learn to whistle 'em so that they follow you home and give themselves up. Been in the charge-room yet?"

"They never forget that," said Wilson. "Trespassing, and being found on enclosed land in possession . . ."

He wiped his sleeve across a moist nose.

"There's a thing, Mr. Lancaster."

"Now look," said Lancaster, pointing the butt end of his pen at him, "it can't be your wife this time! To my knowledge she's had three babies in twelve months, and if you say she's going to have another I just won't believe you!"

"It was something I saw," sniffed Wilson, "and it was the night Mr. Maddison was done in. I happened to be walking in

a field near Cap'ain Saunders's house about half-past twelve—
that's in the morning, after midnight . . ."

"Let's have it, Wilson!"

Wilson rubbed his now-polished nose on the back of a grimy
hand. "Don't know as I ought to say anything, really. Perhaps
better think it over when I've plenty of time to spare in the cell,
and then see you when I come out. It don't do to talk out of
school. Might get somebody into trouble, like as not."

Lancaster sighed.

"These charges ever get put aside and lost?" Wilson asked
hopefully.

Lancaster glanced at Knollis, who was wearing a faint smile.
"Well, you aren't sure of going down the line, Wilson. The mag-
istrates take the case, you know. They'll discharge you if they
think there isn't sufficient evidence. You should know the rest!
You've had nearly as much experience as I have!"

"Who provides the evidence, sir?"

"Police-constable Robinson, in this instance."

Wilson looked at his huge-booted feet.

"If he was to get mixed-up, sir, and forget something . . ."

"He won't," said Lancaster.

Wilson sniffed. "According to the law I ain't expected to say
anything that might get me in deeper, am I? I mean, if what I
was going to tell you was likely to get me up on another do like
tonight's, I'd be a mug, wouldn't I?"

Lancaster restrained himself, admirably. "You aren't bound
to say a thing," he said. "You've been cautioned more than once.
Don't stall!"

Wilson turned away from the desk, and walked slowly toward
the door where Robinson was waiting for him.

"Not a bad gentleman, wasn't Mr. Maddison. Bought me
more than one drink in his tap-room in his time—"

"And he had more than one rabbit from you in his time!"
interrupted Robinson. "Used to leave them on the bench in his
garage, didn't you? Skinned, gutted, and jointed all ready for
the oven."

Wilson sniffed again. He turned to cock an appraising eye at Knollis and Lancaster.

"Reckon I know a couple of gents when I see 'em, gents as wouldn't rub it too hard into a man that's been caught unfairly."

"Thanks," said Lancaster.

"It isn't that I want the coneys," said Wilson. "It's the sport o' the thing. I can't leave it alone. Sort of pitting my brains against coneys same as you do against criminals. There's nothing wrong in it, it's just that the law's against it. I'd still like to creep up behind one and grab him by the ear'oles. That would be something!"

"I'd like to be there when you do it!" said Robinson.

"I wasn't talking to you," Wilson said over his shoulder. He made his way back to the desk, and looked Knollis straight in the eye.

"It was Sunday night. The church clock struck half-past a few minutes afterwards. I was in the field behind Major Oliver's house, and seen somebody coming across from the gate on Woodstock Lane, so I got down in the ditch. He went past me so close that I could smell him—"

"Mr. Maddison was a cleanly man!" Lancaster said reprovingly.

"Men have scent same as animals, sir," replied Wilson. "Anyway, who said it was Mr. Maddison?"

"Your trick," said Lancaster with a shrug.

"It was Mr. Maddison," sniffed Wilson. "He went on towards the house, and I went after him. He got over the fence behind the summer-house, and went down the path towards the house. So did I. The front door was wide open, and I could see Cap'ain Saunders walking about inside. Mr. Maddison called to him, and he came to the door. Then he pushed past him and took something from a low table, held it up, and threw it down again."

"That would be the hall chest," said Lancaster.

"Well, there was a bit more nattering, and then they shook hands, and Mr. Maddison went back the way he came."

"You followed him?"

"Yes, sir. He'd got a lady's bike against the gate, and he went off on it."

"See anybody else?" asked Lancaster.

Wilson smiled craftily. "Expect me to have seen somebody else, sir?"

"We wouldn't be surprised," said Lancaster. "Who was it?"

"The major, trying to hide behind a tree and watch Mr. Maddison."

Knollis had been listening keenly, his arms folded on the desk. He pushed his head forward on his shoulders, and asked a question in a crisp tone.

"Where did Major Oliver go?"

"I didn't say I watched him, sir!"

"But you did," said Knollis. "You wanted to know what it was all about, and so you watched the major as you had watched Mr. Madddison? Right?"

Wilson sighed. "You're right, sir. Of course I watched him. He hopped over the gate opposite, and went across the field that comes out at the elbow on Uppercroft Lane."

"And then . . . ?"

Wilson shook his head. "I don't follow people on hard roads, sir. It makes a noise."

"But which direction did he take? Did he go on to the village, or return to the foot of the lane?"

"He kept going forward towards the Fox, sir."

"And you?"

"I doubled back over the fields to Ell Wood. I'd heard that Mr. Robinson might be looking for me."

"Where were you that night, Robinson?" asked Knollis.

Robinson gave a rueful smile. "I'd rather not answer that just now, sir," he said. Then he stared, and said: "Oh, I see!"

"What is it, Robinson?" asked Lancaster.

"Done with Wilson, sir?"

"Er—yes, I think so."

Robinson led him to the corridor and handed him over to another officer. He returned to the desk. "I got tipped off about

Wilson, sir. On Sunday night, I mean. I was told he was going to work Burnaby Wood, and that's where I went."

"Well?"

"You know the district, sir. Burnaby's on the other side of the valley."

"It is," said Lancaster.

"It was Major Oliver who tipped me off," said Robinson. "Saw him in the village earlier that night. I was on ten to six on Sunday, so I went into the Fox for a drink and a bottle of stout for my wife. The major was in the long bar. He bought me a pint, and said he'd heard something that might interest me. He told me he'd overheard Wilson and his pal, Fletcher talking, and Wilson said he had something on across at Burnaby."

"Any reason why Major Oliver should ever tip you off about Wilson?" Knollis asked.

"He had his poultry run cleared last Christmas, sir. Wilson was suspected, but we couldn't get a thing on him. We think he'd fixed up the sale of them in advance, and had a van waiting to pick them up as he handed them out."

"So Major Oliver is prejudiced against Wilson?"

"That's putting it mildly, sir."

"What time did you go to the Fox?"

"About eight o'clock, sir."

"They open at—what time?"

"Seven, sir. It was Sunday."

Knollis looked at Lancaster. "Think we should let Robinson make the rest of the enquiries?"

"It will look less obvious," said Lancaster. "All Teverby will soon know we've got Wilson, so if Robinson carries on it will look as if he's only interested in the poaching. Yes, I should do that, Robinson. Find out whether Wilson and Fletcher actually were in the Fox that night—before eight."

"You think Major Oliver was ribbing me, sir?"

"We'll call it that for the time being," said Lancaster. "Think it out for yourself!"

"You've heard everything Wilson told us," added Knollis. "Think hard, Robinson!"

Robinson walked to the door and opened it. He paused for a moment and said "Oh!" before closing the door behind him.

"The penny dropped with a resounding tinkle, as the novelists say," laughed Knollis.

"The poor devil's been up all night," said Lancaster. "Remember those days?"

"Heaven forbid," said Knollis. "Anyway, we're getting something to work on at last. So Maddison paid a late call on Saunders, and Oliver followed Maddison back to the village! Those facts are interesting. There was nothing wrong with the medical evidence, was there? It isn't possible that Maddison was murdered earlier?"

"The cellar is considerably cooler than the outside air at this time of the year," said Lancaster, "so we can say he wasn't killed elsewhere and moved into the cellar. It is possible that Oliver stayed on the premises all night. And on the face of it he deliberately got Robinson out of the way. All we can do now is wait for Robinson's report. See, we go out to the brewery this morning, don't we?"

He stretched himself. "I had a rotten night. Darned if I could get into a decent, sound sleep. I had Maddison on my mind all night. You ever get like that?"

"You do the worrying, and I'll do the sleeping," said Knollis with a smile. "Once I get in bed I go unconscious."

At half-past ten Lancaster swung the car into the parking ground of the Bramfield Brewery, and he and Knollis went in search of the managing director.

"We're investigating Mr. Michael Maddison's death," Knollis explained to the portly director, "and there are a few points you can probably clear up for us."

"Anything I can do, you know . . ."

"Maddison has been a tenant—how long?"

"Three years, Inspector, and one of the best men we've had. He possessed ideas and drive. He's added hundreds of pounds to the value of the Fox. Pity it couldn't have been one of our other tenants. I could do with a few of them being murdered off!"

"Can you explain how Maddison obtained the tenancy in view of the fact that he had no previous experience?" asked Knollis.

"But he had experience!"

Knollis's eyebrows went up. "He had? We didn't know that."

The director nodded his head toward his table. "Got his papers out now, as a matter of fact. He had a little place outside Woking for about two years. Oh, you needn't query that. He was soundly vouched for. One of my fellow directors sponsored him, so there's no doubt about it."

"Now I wonder who that could be?" Lancaster wondered aloud.

"You know him well enough. Major Oliver—he lives out at Teverby."

Lancaster whistled. "Oliver vouched for him!"

"Nothing wrong there, surely?"

Lancaster caught Knollis's eye. "Er—no, of course not. I didn't know Oliver had shares in the company, that's what surprised me."

"What was the name of the inn outside Woking?" asked Knollis. "I didn't catch it."

The director reached for the Maddison file and thumbed the leaves. "Here we are. *The Thorns i' The Hedge.* By what Oliver told me, it's a little wayside pub that's well-known to travellers in that part of the world."

"Didn't Major Oliver come from that part of the world, sir?" asked Knollis.

"Yes, I believe he did. Wasn't it Guildford?"

"Ready, Lancaster?" said Knollis.

On the way home it was Lancaster who asked the questions, and Knollis who evaded them, but once back in the office he rang Rhoda Maddison.

"What was the name of the house you lived in at Woking?" he asked. "The Thorns, Wayside Lane, West Green. Thank you. Now, Miss Maddison, did your brother buy or rent the house? May I have the name and address of the house agent? Yes, I've got that down, thank you."

He closed the call and pushed the note pad toward Lancaster. "Now we want those people on the line and we'll know just a wee bit more or considerably less than we did!"

Seven minutes later he replaced the receiver for the second time, and smiled at Lancaster. "That's that! Care to guess who owns the house at Woking?"

"Major Oliver!"

"Top marks!"

Knollis pulled the lobe of his ear thoughtfully, but before he had time to make any further remark Robinson came into the office, looking pleased with himself.

"Soon settled that sir! Neither Wilson nor Fletcher were in the Fox on Sunday night. Fletcher was in the Wain all through the session, and Wilson stayed home, being broke to the wide."

"So Oliver twisted you," Lancaster murmured.

"And cost me three hours of my own time," grumbled Robinson. "I stayed on in the hope of catching him—that's why I was outside the Fox when Rose Cromwell was getting the wind up over Mr. Maddison's absence."

Lancaster glanced up in surprise. "You did that? Good man! Now you can try something else. You can see what happened, can't you! Oliver deliberately wangled you into Burnaby Wood to keep you away from Ell Wood and district. See if you can find the reason. Find out whether anyone else was out in the early hours of the morning. You're a key man from this minute."

"Sir," said Robinson, and was gone.

"Suppose we'd better settle down and map out a plan of campaign," suggested Lancaster.

Knollis did not agree. "We've other work to do before darkness falls. Get the necessary authority and a digging squad. We're going to turn the Fox inside out, search the drains, and dig up the garden. Maddison's arrows, and his papers, must be found before we can advance another step."

"If ever I want my garden digging really well," said Lancaster, "I'll spread the rumour that there's a body buried there."

He glanced at Knollis, absently breaking a cigarette into small pieces and shredding them in the ash-tray. "You didn't know that I swiped three firsts with my celery at the Police Show, did you?"

"No," replied Knollis. "The more I think about it, the more it looks like blackmail to me."

Lancaster clicked his tongue, and turned away with disgust written across his fresh-complexioned features. "Oh, give me strength to endure!"

Chapter XI
THE DEDUCTIONS OF LANCASTER

By NIGHTFALL the inn had been searched from attics to cellars, and the garden double-dug by a squad of constables with more energy than enthusiasm. Lancaster left the rose-beds after examining the bushes and standards and finding none that had wilted as a result of being moved or replanted. In the house, Knollis and Lancaster, with Sergeant MacFarlane, assisting, had looked in every drawer and cupboard, tested furniture for secret hiding-places and floors for loose boards, and even sent two detective-officers into the be-cobwebbed false roof with powerful torches.

While all this was happening, Rhoda Maddison had gone about her normal routine smiling outwardly, and as calm as ever. She provided tea for all concerned in the search at half-past four, laying tables in the saloon as if she was entertaining the village cricket team, a courtesy that embarrassed Knollis and Lancaster.

"It's like a condemned man helping the hangman by putting the rope round his own neck," said Lancaster. "She knows darn well we're gunning for her or her relatives or acquaintances, and she showers kindnesses on us!"

Knollis smiled wryly. "It means she feels safe, Lancaster. It's her way of expressing her own satisfaction—plus, probably, a trace of sarcasm. Still, that's a side-issue. I can understand Maddison's papers being safely hidden from us, but the arrows are a different matter. Six arrows, twenty-eight inches long, are not easy things to hide!"

"I wonder if she's carrying the papers round with her?" mused Lancaster. "What about sending for a police-woman to search her?"

Knollis did not agree. "I think not," he said. "Let's leave her alone for a day or so, and then pounce on her again. She'll think she's safe after this performance, and may hide them again. For the arrows, I'm wondering . . . !"

"Wondering what?"

Knollis narrowed his eyes. "There's a persistent picture in my mind of Gillian Saunders biking over the hill from Maunsby, bent double over the handlebars racing against time . . ."

Lancaster waved the idea away. "She was wanting to get back before the Denby household was awake."

"I thought that at first," said Knollis, "but now I'm not so sure. Suppose she got back after Mrs. Denby and Sally were up? She could have got away with it quite easily by saying she wanted this or that from home before going to work, and so she had borrowed the cycle without disturbing anyone. Our original idea was that she was racing to get back to Maunsby. Now I'm wondering if she was racing to get there for a specific reason?"

"To catch Maddison in the cellar," said Lancaster.

"No," replied Knollis. "That's wrong! Didn't Rhoda Maddison tell you that her brother rose at half-past seven each morning?"

"Ye—es, that's right! She did."

"Now so far as we know, neither she nor Saunders knew about the celluloid strip. That's their story, anyway."

"That's so," agreed Lancaster.

"So why was she racing to get to the inn? Think that one out. If her story was true she couldn't get into the inn before Maddison rose at half-past seven."

"Well?"

"Suppose she was trying to intercept someone else who was going to the inn?"

Lancaster stared "But that can only mean her husband, Saunders!"

Knollis smiled. "It's an idea, isn't it?"

Lancaster hummed a few bars of a popular waltz, and scratched his head. "You know, Knollis," he said slowly, "there's another angle. If Rhoda fixed the celluloid strip it was for Saunders' benefit, and not her own. She was already in the house, but Saunders had to be provided with a means of entry. Now in that case we can assume he told Gillian."

"Yes," Knollis admitted reluctantly. "That's true."

"In that case she knew, as she cycled from Maunsby, that she could get in the house!"

"That's also true," said Knollis, "and puts a different complexion on the matter. Yes, you're correct, Lancaster. Saunders was the only person who knew the intentions of both parties."

"As for the arrows," said Lancaster, "well, what happened to the two hunting arrows after they were stolen?"

"They were put in the—oh lord, yes! I never thought about that!"

"The only place we haven't looked into," said Lancaster. "Shall we go indoors?"

He strode from the garden to the lobby and took the golf bag from its hook. "Here we are, my friend! Seven prettily feathered arrows."

Knollis snorted his impatience with himself. "Never entered my head. Nice work, Lancaster!"

"We'd better take the bag as it is," said Lancaster. "There might be a few decent prints on them. Do you know what I think happened?"

"Let's hear it."

"I think Gillian found the body," Lancaster said in a low voice, and glanced over his shoulder to make sure he was not being overheard. "I think she found her uncle and faked the job. And I'll bet you a bob she secretly thinks her husband did it! I've been puzzled over one thing since I first heard of it—Gillian spending the night with Sally Denby. Why should she?"

He took Knollis's elbow and led him out into the village street, away from the possibility of being eavesdropped.

"See what I mean, Knollis. They'd only been married a few days, and it wasn't natural for her to be away from her husband and her real home. It wasn't necessary for her to stay in town. Saunders could quite easily have run her to the road junction next morning, and with little real risk of them being seen. She could have caught a bus into town from there, and no one any the wiser if she had pitched the story, as she did, about staying with the Denby girl. Now then, here's the crux of the matter! Who decided she wasn't to stay with her husband? Not herself, I'll be bound! Ask yourself that one and see what answer you get!"

"Must have been Saunders," said Knollis with a sign.

"That's what I think. What is the inevitable conclusion Gillian then reaches? That Saunders wants her out of the way for some reason or other, and that he is going to the Fox during the night and doesn't want her to know. Maddison is a menace to her, and her husband intends removing the menace. We're now back to your mental picture of her racing over the hill from town. She arrives a few minutes before half-past, if we can rely on the lorry driver's evidence, which I think we can. Now then, doesn't that mean that she arrived just before Maddison was killed, as he was being killed, or just after he was killed?"

"It does," said Knollis. "You've certainly been thinking, Lancaster!"

He stood on the edge of the pavement for several minutes, his forehead puckered, and his hands thrust deep into his jacket pockets.

"We'll take her back to headquarters and grill her," he said at last. "I'll collect her, while you tell MacFarlane to smuggle the golf bag into the second car and follow us home. We must have a showdown with the young lady. I said she was a little fox, and she is. She has a good and nimble brain, Lancaster!"

Gillian created a scene in the lobby before allowing herself to be taken to the car, and almost tearfully asked Rose Cromwell to telephone Saunders and tell him what was happening to her. Rhoda meanwhile stood with her back to the wall, her features expressionless, and her white hands folded beneath her virginal breasts.

"Aunt Rhoda!" pleaded Gillian. "You'll see that Harry is told?"

"Rose is at liberty to 'phone him if she wishes," Rhoda replied coldly. "He's yours, not mine! You've never accepted my advice and guidance, so you must sort out your own tangles. Assuming these gentlemen don't detain you at the police station you'd better return to Ellwood House. I have washed my hands of you. I shall have your things sent down for you immediately. The name of the house cannot be allowed to suffer because you have—so evidently—allowed yourself to become associated with the murderer of your own uncle!"

"Aunt Rhoda!" exclaimed Gillian.

"She is not suspected of anything, and neither is anyone else at the moment," Knollis pointed out firmly.

"I will not have her back," snapped Rhoda. "Rose, when you've 'phoned Captain Saunders I wish you to pack Mrs. Saunders' clothes and have them taken to Ellwood House!"

"Mrs. Saunders, ma'am?"

"*Née* Gillian Maddison," smirked Rhoda. "You can tell that to the village!" She walked to the sitting-room, closing the door firmly behind her.

"You know," said Lancaster, "that's the best thing that could have happened to you, Mrs. Saunders. Sorry for the way it's come about, but it is impossible to talk privately in this place. We'll run you home to your husband when we're through."

Gillian ignored him. She stared at the closed door, her tiny fists clenched. "I'll get her yet!" she exclaimed, and then allowed Lancaster to lead her out to the waiting car.

She was still in a temper when taken into Lancaster's office. She walked straight to the window, and stood with her back towards them, a slim and tense figure in her cream blouse and grey costume.

"Now come, Mrs. Saunders," Knollis said gently; "let's get this interview over, please."

"I've nothing to tell you—other than what I've already told you," she replied.

"Maybe not, but you've plenty to explain," said Knollis.

She turned back into the room, and thrust her fingers wildly through the wealth of auburn hair. "I won't say a word until my husband arrives."

"Pity," commented Knollis, "because I don't think you'll like your husband to hear what you *will* have to say to us."

"Why not, indeed?" she demanded. "What can I have to say?"

Knollis perched himself on the corner of Lancaster's desk. "You suspect your husband of murdering your uncle Michael."

Gillian started. "I—why, the idea never entered my head! Why on earth should I suspect him. What cause had he to murder Michael?"

"You don't think he had?"

"I'm sure he hadn't!"

"Then why were you racing to Teverby at twenty past six on Monday morning—ten minutes before he was killed in his own cellar?"

Knollis signalled Lancaster to take over. After all, it was his notion, and Knollis was nothing if not fair.

"You see, Mrs. Saunders," said Lancaster, "it seems to us that you arrived at the inn just as your uncle was being murdered. You might even have witnessed his death!"

She drew her upper lip between her teeth and stared wonderingly at Lancaster.

"Our job is to find things out," said Lancaster, "and we are satisfied that it was you racing over the hill from Maunsby. You took Miss Denby's bike from the shed after her father had gone to work. The lorry driver gave a very accurate description of you—and you did refuse the identification parade, you know!"

He watched her closely for a moment, and added: "All the evidence seems to prove that your husband was safely in bed."

Gillian still refused to speak, and kept a firm grip on her lip.

"Your husband told you about the celluloid strip which had been fixed to the latch-box," went on Lancaster, "and explained why it gave free access to the house. Now why, I wonder, did you return to the inn at that time of the morning? To fetch a clean handkerchief? To powder your nose? Or perhaps it was to try to prevent a crime being committed? You did go down the cellar, of course," he said in a tone that suggested he knew it as a fact.

Gillian sought a nearby chair, and gripped her clasped hands between her knees. In a low voice she said: "Michael was dying . . ."

Lancaster sighed his relief, and looked across at Knollis, idly swinging his legs from the desk, and apparently only mildly interested in the dramatic admission.

"There was someone in the cellar," said Gillian. "There's a wine store off it, and the door is usually kept open. This morning it was closed, and I heard a slight movement behind it. Michael was dying. His eyes were open, and I'm sure he knew me, but he couldn't speak . . . blood was coming from his mouth. I wanted to know who was beyond the door, but I—well, I daren't look."

"Afraid of being attacked, of course," said Lancaster.

Gillian looked at him, frowning queerly. She shook her head. "Afraid, yes, but not of that. I was afraid of—of . . ."

"Discovering the identity of your uncle's murderer," suggested Knollis.

"Yes," she replied. "Yes, that was it. You see, it might have been—might have been . . ."

"We understand, Mrs. Saunders," said Lancaster. "What did you do?"

"I ran from the house and went straight to my husband."

Lancaster clicked his tongue. "That means he knew at least two hours before your aunt 'phoned him! Now why didn't he report it to us straight away? Still, that can wait. But before you went to your husband, Mrs. Saunders. What did you do before that? How much moving and re-arranging did you do in the cellar?"

Gillian gave him a curious stare. "I didn't touch a thing, Inspector."

"Your uncle's arrows? They were in the cellar?"

"Those he bought from Cowan? Yes, they were lying across one of the barrels."

"You didn't touch them?"

She shook her auburn head. "No, Inspector. I did not."

"The target cupboard doors?"

"They were wide open. It was the first time I had seen inside it."

"Now for the lights," said Lancaster.

"Only the one was switched on, and that the one focused on the target."

"Why did you go down the cellar at all?" asked Lancaster.

"The door was open, and I could hear someone moving about. I naturally thought it was Michael, and went down to him."

"How on earth were you going to explain your presence at that time of the morning?"

"I hadn't thought about it," said Gillian.

"For the time being," said Lancaster, "we'll ignore your reason for being there at all at that time of the day. I'd like to go back to the evening when your husband's hunting arrows were stolen from the bar. Haven't you really any idea who took them?"

"Honestly, I haven't! I—"

The door opened, and Saunders strode in.

"What the dickens is happening?" he demanded. "Is my wife to take lodgings with you?"

"Not yet," said Lancaster. "What I want to know is how you got in my office like this?"

"I just walked through and no one made any attempt to stop me," Saunders retorted. "And they wouldn't have stopped me if they'd tried!"

"Interesting to be told that," said Lancaster. "You got down the cellar at the Fox in the same way last Monday morning. It must be a gift!"

Saunders waved a hand toward his wife. "What have you brought her here for?"

"My dear fellow," said Lancaster, "you must realise it is impossible to talk at the inn, and she has vital evidence to give us."

Gillian smiled wanly at her husband. "I've told them all of it, Harry, right from the beginning—how I found Michael dead, and how I came to you, and—"

"Just a moment, please," said Lancaster. "We know that one. Your husband can tell his own story, not the one you're trying to tell him first. Now, Captain Saunders, suppose you tell us what you know, and we'll see if it matches your wife's story."

Saunders gave his characteristic shrug. "All I have to tell you is that my wife came throwing pebbles at my window at a quarter to seven in the morning. I let her in, and she told me she'd found Michael Maddison dead or dying in the cellar at the Fox. I realised that if anyone knew she was there she'd be suspected, so I didn't even bother to dress, but just pulled my overcoat over my dressing-gown and rushed her back to town. I pushed the car from the garage to the road to avoid waking Bates, and then we wedged the bike in the boot of the car and drove like blazes to Canal Street. It was deserted, so I decanted the bike round the corner, on the tow-path, told Gillian to keep silent, and not to worry, and came home and went to bed again. Bates's room is at the other end of the house, and at the back, so I don't think he heard anything—he's said nothing, anyway."

"Any idea why your wife should have been at the inn at that time of the morning?" asked Knollis, sliding from the desk and advancing across the room.

Saunders scratched his head. "I haven't even bothered to ask her that. I took it for granted she had her reasons, and would tell me if she wanted me to know. I was brought up to mind my own business. I can only assume she wanted a look at her uncle's private papers and so on."

"That was it!" Gillian said too eagerly.

Knollis decided to let her get away with the explanation, at any rate in front of her husband.

"How did she expect to be able to get into the place?" asked Knollis.

Saunders gave a long slow smile, and Knollis both feared and knew the answer before Saunders gave it.

"She is old enough to have a latch key," he replied, and the expression on his tanned face revealed only too well his knowledge that he had sunk both Knollis and Lancaster without trace.

Lancaster turned away to hide his chagrin.

"The simple answer it is which turneth away suspicion," smiled Saunders. "Seriously though, we had to find why Maddison objected to her marriage—with anyone, not just me—and what he could do about it, and that had to be done before we could openly declare that we were man and wife and tell Maddison to go to blazes. Maddison was her guardian, and for all we knew he might have been controlling money that belonged to her. It's my belief that he was doing so, and my further belief that he was using it, so that he was afraid of discovery, and afraid of losing control if she married after she was twenty-one and his guardianship ceased."

"The penny is dropping," nodded Knollis.

He turned to Gillian. "Can you tell me who owned the Surrey house you lived in for two years?"

She shook her head. "I know the rent was paid quarterly to an agent in Woking, but no more."

"Any idea in what business your uncle was engaged while down there? He was in business, wasn't he?"

"I honestly don't know, Inspector. We never asked him. He went out nearly every weekday morning about ten o'clock, but we never asked questions—Michael never answered questions," Gillian said grimly.

"You see," said Saunders, "he was so determined on Rhoda and Gillian not marrying that he raised my suspicions. I could have understood the objection or ban on Gillian, since she was still in his care, but not on Rhoda as well. I began to wonder if he was a real bad lot. You see, when he took over the care of Gillian she was too young to know what was being arranged—or else she wasn't told, so if he was twisting her there was a sound reason for his marriage ban. The question now arose in my mind; was he also twisting Rhoda?"

"How?" asked Lancaster.

"Well, was there money on both sides of the family? Had his parents left any money in some kind of trust for Rhoda? Had Gillian's parents done the same thing? And consequently I asked myself if Maddison had parcelled up both lots for himself, knowing that his only means of keeping his secret was the prevention of marriage for either of the girls?"

"That is definitely an idea," said Knollis. "Done anything about it?"

"I've written to the solicitors who drew up the deed referring to Gillian."

"There's a point," murmured Lancaster. "What was he doing with the money, assuming there was any, and assuming he'd got hold of it?"

"That is something to be discovered when we know whether there was any," said Saunders. "Suppose you people ask a few questions of his bank? We can estimate his earnings at the Fox. Anything over and above that . . ."

"Thanks for the hints," said Knollis seriously. "The arrows are interesting us."

Saunders raised his shoulders. "I haven't a clue."

"I don't mean yours," said Knollis. "I mean the set of seven your wife saw in the Cellar when she discovered her uncle."

Saunders turned to Gillian. "They were there?"

"On the top of a barrel—and I haven't told you this before, but there was someone hiding in the wine store."

"Oh!" exclaimed Saunders. "Did you—"

"Go to see if your aunt was in bed? Is that what you were going to say, Captain Saunders?" Knollis interrupted.

Saunders nodded. "Yes, it was."

"I didn't," said Gillian. "I was afraid . . . and got down to you as quickly as the bike would take me."

"Naturally," said Saunders, with a fond glance at his wife.

"Not so much because she wanted you to look after her," said Knollis.

Saunders cocked an enquiring eye. "What the devil do you mean, Inspector?"

"She wanted to make sure it wasn't you behind the door."

Saunders looked down at his wife, a bent figure in the chair. "You were suspecting me of bumping off Michael?"

Gillian lowered her head.

Saunders laughed shortly. "Serves me right, of course. I'd suggested it in a rash moment, saying it would save a lot of trouble. So that's why you chased over from Maunsby, Gillian? To stop me from lying in wait for Michael . . . ?"

"Ye—es," she admitted reluctantly. "You see, Harry, you wouldn't let me stay with you, and I thought—I wondered . . ."

"You made her spend the night in Maunsby," said Lancaster, "and that peculiar decision might have hanged you—either of you, or both of you."

Saunders stalked across the office and came back to face them. "It was a sensible decision considering the circumstances. It was safe enough to have her there at night, but I'd have been taking her to business at half-past eight, and running into milk-men, and newsboys, and the postman, and farm workers— to say nothing of the mysterious yoga-practising Major Oliver. He's always on the prowl in Woodstock Lane, and if he'd seen us together he'd have been across at the Fox five minutes later to tell Rhoda!"

He clicked his tongue at Gillian. "You know, darling, a wife is supposed to believe her husband to be above common murdering!"

Gillian was sobbing quietly into her handkerchief.

"Take her home," said Lancaster briefly.

Knollis was sitting with his feet up on the desk when Lancaster returned from the door, tapping his knees with an ebony ruler.

"We've made a lot of mistakes, Lancaster!"

"You're telling me!"

"One of them concerns the celluloid strip. It couldn't have been either Rhoda or Gillian Maddison who fixed it."

"And why not?" demanded Lancaster.

"Look," said Knollis; "Rhoda could have supplied Saunders with a key?"

"I suppose so."

"And Gillian could have done the same?"

"Yes, of course."

"The strip," said Knollis in his best lecturing voice, "was obviously fixed by someone who couldn't obtain a key. The odds are in favour of it having been fitted while the inn was open, and fairly late at night, with dusk falling. It was also a sudden decision, made almost on the spur of the moment. Just to complete the bill, I'll say it was fixed the night the arrows were stolen, or perhaps the next one. The material was taken from Rhoda Maddison's saddle-bag, probably with a screwdriver from the same source. Now we must find out at what time the coach party left that night, and at what time Major Oliver went home."

"Major Oliver?" exclaimed Lancaster. "Why Major Oliver? Isn't it more reasonable to assume that Rhoda Maddison fixed the job herself, to make it look like an outside job?"

"You think that, Lancaster?" asked Knollis.

"I most certainly do!"

"Oh well!" said Knollis.

Chapter XII
THE EVIDENCE OF ROBERTS

LANCASTER'S FIRST visitor the next morning was Roberts, late cellarman of the Fox, and Lancaster decided to see him at once.

Roberts waddled into the office, a tubby, red-faced little man who was looking considerably worried. He stood aimlessly in the middle off the floor as if wondering whether to curtsey, bow, or shake hands with the Inspector.

Lancaster nodded toward a chair. "Make yourself comfortable, Mr. Roberts. What can I do for you?"

Roberts ignored the invitation, and scratched his ear doubtfully. "I don't know that anybody can do anything for me, but there's nothing to be lost by trying. It's this Mr. Maddison affair, sir. Everybody in the village's treating me as if I'd done him in!"

"And you didn't," said Lancaster.

"I didn't, sir. You should know that."

"We do know it," Lancaster assured him. "So far as we are concerned you are the most innocent man in Teverby village."

Roberts drew a great breath. "It's nice to hear you say that, sir."

Knollis walked in, said good morning, and flung his hat on the hook with an expert hand.

"This is Mr. Roberts, the late cellarman of the Fox," explained Lancaster. "He's in gossip trouble."

"It's the people in the village," complained Roberts. "They treat me as if I'd done Mr. Maddison in myself."

"You've nothing to worry about," smiled Knollis. "We completed our enquiries regarding you only a few hours after Maddison died. As for the villagers, you must be patient, Mr. Roberts, and remember you are living in a Christian country rife with understanding and charity, where people invent explanations suitable to themselves if they can't find the true one."

"How horribly cynical!" Lancaster retorted.

"True, nevertheless," said Knollis. "I'm sorry for you, Mr. Roberts, but there's nothing any of us can do at the moment. I'm afraid you must stick it out until we've got our man."

"Still in work?" asked Lancaster.

"I am, and I'm not, sir. Mr. Ellis at the Wain has had to ask me to keep away for a time. His customers seem to think I'm putting poison in every pint I draw for them."

"What are you doing with your time?"

"Walking the country lanes most of the time," grunted Roberts, "trying to think who could have done him in!"

"Who *could* have killed him?" asked Lancaster. "Any ideas?"

Roberts looked at him with a vague air of bewilderment. "That's what's puzzling me, sir!"

"Did you like the man?"

Roberts sought for words, and waved his hands aimlessly as if trying to conjure them into existence. "Well, yes, I did. I don't know what came over him that night. I know he was the boss, but we were always good pals—and then he simply turned queer all at once and was as nasty as anybody could be."

"He'd nothing against you, really," Knollis said softly. "He wanted the cellar to himself for certain reasons, and had to get rid of you. I take it you're not sorry he's gone?"

"But I am, sir," Roberts protested. "I tell you, he was all right except for that night. He always paid me more than we'd arranged, and on busy nights he often gave me a tip when we'd closed. He was a gent to me!"

"What was he like with the two women?" asked Lancaster curiously.

Roberts shuffled his feet. "Well, he *was* different with them. He was a man's man, you see, and hadn't much time for women. He thought they were inferior to men. He never told them a thing, because he said they couldn't keep their traps shut even about things that concerned their own welfare, and he said they were hopeless with money matters. He was pleasant with them, but he always sort of kept a fence between him and them. Once, for instance, I heard Miss Rhoda suggest something or other for the pub, and he said if it was a good idea he'd think it up himself, and it would be better if she'd attend to the oven and the sink. Snubbed her proper, he did."

"Was there anyone else in the lobby when you had the row with him?" asked Knollis.

"No-o, not exactly in the lobby, sir. Miss Rhoda looked in to see what was happening, and backed into the bar again. Oh, and Major Oliver came in through the swing doors, and he backed out as well."

"Where was Miss Gillian?"

"Serving in the smoke-room."

"Tell me, Mr. Roberts, did you see the hunting arrows on the shelf behind the bar?"

"Yes, sir, and they were under the spirit optics."

"Now think," said Knollis. "Do you think they would have been reached—could have been reached—from the smoke-room serving hatch?"

"Not unless anybody had a heck of a long arm, sir. I think I know what could have happened . . . !"

"Go on then."

"That half-door is fastened by a small bolt which is just under the shelf of the door. Anybody standing there waiting for an order could have slipped the bolt without being seen, and moved just far enough into the bar to get at the arrows without anybody noticing."

"And what could he have done with the arrows?" asked Knollis. "He couldn't take them in to the smoke-room while Captain Saunders was there, could he?"

"It was a pretty busy hour, sir. About thirty people had piled in from a coach. My guess is that the arrows were pushed under the bottom shelf until later in the evening."

"What makes you think that?"

"Well, they'd be a bit con—conspicuous to carry away there and then, wouldn't they? Isn't that what you were getting at yourself?"

"It was," admitted Knollis. "Those, then, are the two possibilities."

"I only mentioned one, sir."

"Yes, I know you did," said Knollis. "The other one is in my mind."

He stared vacantly at Lancaster for a moment, and turned to Roberts. "See, what is on the shelf under the one on which the wine and spirit bottles are arranged?"

"Glasses, sir. Two rows of them."

"They were used that night?"

"I can't say, sir, but I'll guess they weren't. There'd be enough under the bar counter to fill all the orders needed that night. We had to get a sunny weekend, and the lawn full of people to use those."

"So the arrows might have been slipped behind the glasses? Do you agree, Mr. Roberts?"

"The bottom shelf, sir," Roberts persisted. "It comes to about three inches of the floor—enough room being left for cleaning, and as far as I can see the only place where they wouldn't have been noticed was under that bottom shelf."

"Who took 'em, Roberts?" asked Lancaster. "You must have your own ideas."

"One of the ladies, sir, and my guess is the old one. Rose Cromwell has told me there was some sort of a row that night, and Mr. Maddison smacked Miss Rhoda across the mouth and then punched her jaw. She saw the bruise when she got there next morning, and a bit later Miss Rhoda had camouflaged it with paint and powder. He never treated her proper, and I reckon—"

He broke off, and looked at his hands.

"You reckon what?" asked Lancaster.

"Something I've no right to say, sir," Roberts said frankly. "My tongue's running away with me. I'd best be getting home."

"Ah well," said Knollis. "Don't let them get you down. Both the Maddison ladies have a high opinion of you, and wouldn't hear a word said against you. I suppose you know that Miss Gillian is married?"

"Heard it in the Wain last night, sir. Made me wonder, with her being married to the Captain."

"What made you wonder?" Knollis asked quickly.

"I went for a walk over the fields, and on to Woodstock Lane while making my way to the Wain—I called in for a drink, and the customers can't stop me doing that! Anyway, I saw her coming away from Woodstock House, looking pleased with herself. She passed me on her bike, and didn't seem to notice me. All wrapped up in her thoughts, she was, and laughing about something. She turned right at the foot of the lane, as if going to Ellwood House."

Roberts paused and then said: "It wasn't only that, but she wasn't in mourning. She was wearing a real bright frock, and bending forward to try to fix a big envelope that was in the basket on the handlebars."

Knollis glanced at Lancaster. "Big envelope?"

"Oh, one this size," said Roberts, holding his hands about a foot apart. "There was a seal on it, and she was grinning at it as if it was good news. I couldn't help noticing."

"Was Captain Saunders anywhere in sight?"

"He was in the Wain when I got there. He bought me a drink, and jokingly said it looked as if the Fox had got too hot for both of us."

"Do you think he had just gone in, or had been there for some time?"

"Been in some time, sir," Roberts said. "He drinks whisky, but they hadn't any down there and he'd gone on bottled pale ale. He was pushing his glass forward for a second one, so I'd say he'd been in at least twenty minutes by the way he used to go on at the Fox."

"See anything of Major Oliver during the evening?"

"He came down half an hour later. He said it was too much like a morgue at the Fox, and Mr. Ellis, the Wain landlord, remarked that it was a most unfortunate remark taking everything into consideration."

Knollis turned to the desk for his pen and a sheet of paper. "At what time did you go into the Wain, Mr. Roberts?"

"Twenty-five past eight, sir. It was half-past by the clock, and it's always five minutes fast."

"And you think Saunders had been there since, roughly, eight o'clock?"

"I'd say so, sir."

"And Major Oliver came in at . . . ?"

"Five to nine."

Roberts looked down at the sheet of paper, and asked a question. "Have I put you on to something, sir? I shouldn't like to do Miss Gillian any harm."

"Nothing to get excited about," replied Knollis. "In any case, the sooner we solve this case the sooner you are out of the doghouse as far as the villagers are concerned. Stick it out for a few more days, like a good chap. It will help us."

Roberts grimaced, and then his face cleared. "Oh well, sir, if you put it like that. I was going to start a row and hit somebody tonight—just to clear the air."

"Don't do it!" said Knollis. "And please don't say a word about what you've told us this morning."

With Roberts out of the way Knollis asked Lancaster whether the Teverby constable would be on duty.

"How the deuce do I know?" demanded Lancaster. "I don't run the uniformed department."

"Sorry," murmured Knollis. "Can you arrange for a message to be sent to him? Ask him to find out at what time Oliver went in the Fox last night."

Lancaster did the business on the internal telephone, and then swung round on Knollis in a petulant mood. "What next, your lordship?"

"Sit back, put up your feet, and wait," smiled Knollis. "If you must work, then fix another search warrant."

"For the Fox?"

"Ellwood House."

"Why there?"

"Lancaster!" Knollis protested. "What on earth do you think the girl had in the bike-basket? Fly-papers?"

"Oh!" exclaimed Lancaster.

"Don't you see the thing?" snapped Knollis. "It was Oliver who whipped Maddison's papers! It was Oliver who took the celluloid panel from Rhoda Maddison's saddle-bag and cut it to shape and screwed it into the latch-box. I said last night it was someone who couldn't get hold of a key by legitimate means. Oliver couldn't, and so he used the professional housebreaker's trick, and when Saunders let himself in that night of nights when he and his wife did the rope trick—well, he was too late. Oliver must have dodged in early, and in fact he must have been in the house while Rhoda was searching Gillian's room, or while Gillian was roping her aunt's door. There's no other explanation for it. I can't suggest why he should do it, but there's no other explanation of the facts!"

"Which means Gillian repaid the compliment last night," mused Lancaster.

The telephone rang, and Lancaster took the call. "Robinson," he said two minutes later. "He's had the Cromwell woman on the blower. The major was in the Fox shortly after seven, and came away about a quarter to nine."

Knollis pushed back his chair. "I think we'd better call at Ellwood House, and go on to see the major. It's time we had a show-down with these people."

Saunders and Gillian were on the defensive from the moment Knollis and Lancaster walked into the house, and Knollis decided, after eyeing them up and down, to come straight to the point.

"I want to see the documents you took from Major Oliver's house last night, Mrs. Saunders," he said.

Lancaster nodded, to emphasise their determination. Gillian looked away from her husband and moved uncomfortably on the settee.

"I'm afraid we can't oblige," said Saunders. "They happen to be her own property, and were handed to her, quite voluntarily, by Major Oliver. Sorry!"

"At what time did you collect them, Mrs. Saunders?" Knollis asked quietly.

"Oh, it would be eight o'clock," she replied without looking up.

"Major Oliver was in the Fox from seven to a quarter to nine, and spent the remainder of the evening in the Wain," Knollis said in a crisp, official voice.

Saunders walked over to his wife. "You hear that, Gillian?" To Knollis he said: "You're sure of your facts, Inspector?"

"We've clouds of witnesses," said Knollis. "There were other people in the inn, you know!"

Saunders scratched his head, frowned down on his wife's auburn head, and said: "Oh!"

"We're not particularly interested in how your wife got the documents," said Knollis. "That is Major Oliver's business, and he hasn't yet approached us. For the time being we'll be satisfied if we get a glance at whatever was in the large envelope with the red seal."

Saunders shook his head. "I'm sorry, no!"

Lancaster pushed the search warrant under his nose. "You can choose your method, sir!"

Saunders snorted, and tapped his wife on the shoulder, not too lightly. "Did you take the things when he wasn't there, Gillian?"

"Yes," she admitted reluctantly. "I found them in his library."

"What were you doing in his library if he wasn't at home?"

"I went to see him. The door was wide open, and no one answered my knock, so I went in."

"I suppose you knocked with a feather," Saunders said sarcastically.

"The envelope was on the table, and it was addressed to Michael, so I'd more right to it than he had! Then I looked inside, and came home with it as fast as I could. They do concern me, don't they?" she asked defiantly.

"They certainly do," said Saunders, "but I don't like the method of obtaining them. No wonder I thought it queer that he should hand them over. And that raises the question: how did he get hold of them?"

"The question at the moment," Knollis reminded him, "is that we want to see the contents of the envelope, and do we have to use the warrant?"

Saunders shrugged his shoulders. "No, of course not!"

He went to a drawer and handed the envelope to Knollis. "I can save you a lot of trouble by telling you what it adds up to, Inspector. Maddison's father was evidently a wealthy man, and he left a matter of ten thousand pounds to be shared between Rhoda and Gillian's father. In his will—there's a copy in the envelope—he said he had educated Michael up to the hilt, and he must regard the money spent on him as his share. Gillian's father had made his own way, and had never called for help, and Rhoda had never asked for a penny in her life; therefore they were entitled to his money.

"Now, so far as Rhoda was concerned, her father was concerned about her lack of experience with money or anything else, and so he left her share in trust, the interest on the investments to be administered by Michael, according to his discretion, until she eventually married, or otherwise until she was forty years of age."

"Ah!" exclaimed Lancaster, as if a revelation had been declared to him. Knollis merely nodded as if it was no more than he had expected.

"Gillian's father, killed in the air raid," went on Saunders, "left his share, plus what little he had made, to his wife, and on her decease to Gillian and her sister, the estate to be administered by the elder of any surviving male members of the family until each girl reached the age of twenty-one, when the capital became available to them. As Gillian's mother and sister were killed with her father—and Michael was the only male survivor, so he automatically took over her affairs as well. His bank book is here, and we're puzzled, because there isn't any of either Rhoda's or Gillian's money shown in it; no more, in fact, than his receipts as the landlord of the Fox!"

"How much is entailed?" asked Knollis, slipping the documents from the envelope.

"I haven't worked it out yet," replied Saunders. "The lists of investments are there, and there are good ones and bad ones, but I can't see either of them being entitled to less than a fiver a week. How much did he give you, Gillian?"

"Nothing," Gillian said surprisingly. "He kept me, and let me have what I earned—out of which I had to buy my own clothes."

"Wasn't he a stinker?" Saunders asked of no one in particular.

Knollis sorted the documents, and gave the copies of her father's will and the deed of guardianship to Gillian. "The bank book and the rest are obviously the property of your aunt, and we'll see she gets them. One question remains to be asked of you."

"Yes?" Gillian asked in a small voice.

"What was the latest time you were in the sitting-room at the Fox, and looked in the bureau, on the night when it was rifled?"

"Eleven."

"And went to bed . . . how soon after that?"

"Only a few minutes, Inspector. Aunt Rhoda followed me up the stairs, switching the lights off as she came."

"You don't think she went down again?"

"I'm sure she didn't. I heard the usual bathroom noises—the taps running and the cistern refilling."

"And you next went down . . . ?"

"About an hour later, to meet Harry in the passage."

"It sounds a bit of a mystery," said Saunders. "Not in line with Oliver's character at all. I suppose he really did go in the house and take these things?"

"Between your wife going to bed, and going down again to meet you," said Knollis. "That's the obvious answer. Either that, or someone else got them for him."

Saunders grimaced. "There is no other solution, is there? You never know people, do you?"

Gillian suddenly came to life, her eyes excited and eager. "I'd forgotten! Rhoda went back to the sitting-room afterwards—to answer the 'phone call from Harry. She could have cleared the bureau then!"

"That's worth thinking about," Lancaster said quickly. "Suppose she did hand them over to Oliver, Knollis?"

"With what object?"

Gillian interrupted the discussion.

"I'm sure she suspected that Harry and I had got married, and that left her without him, and without anyone to advise or help her. Suppose she turned to Major Oliver? In any case it would have been a good way of showing him she was interested in him. You see, she was determined to marry someone, and I think she was keeping Major Oliver on ice in case Harry didn't propose to her. To ask him for help would be a good move!"

"A feminine angle that hadn't occurred to me," said Knollis. "You may have something there, Mrs. Saunders."

"The helpless little woman appealing to the strong and experienced man of the world," grunted Lancaster.

"Yes, that's it!" said Gillian.

Saunders grimaced again, and rubbed his hand over his brown hair. "Doesn't it just reveal the way in which women wangle men to gain their own ends, eh? They are worth their keep if only for their cunning!"

"Harry!" protested Gillian.

"You've amply demonstrated it, darling," smiled Saunders. "I know you've done all your weird moves in my interests, but whatever you do or don't do in future, please leave out lying, I don't like it!"

"That's right, Mrs. Saunders," said Knollis as he pocketed the envelope and prepared to leave. "Take your husband's advice and don't tell lies. Just stick to murder and you'll be all right!"

"Well!" exclaimed Gillian.

Outside, on Ellwood Road, Lancaster asked: "Was that last remark quite nice, Knollis."

"I don't know yet," Knollis replied blandly. "The more I see of her the less I think about other suspects. She can lie like a trooper, and rationalise like nobody's business; she had everything to gain by her uncle's death, and little to lose providing she kept her head—and she was in the cellar when her uncle was dying! She's the most cunning little fox I've yet met, and utterly amoral. She doesn't know the difference between right and wrong, and will say anything or do anything providing it satisfies her own ends."

Chapter XIII
THE EVIDENCE OF THE BOWYER

KNOLLIS LEFT Ellwood House with the feeling that he had reached an impasse. There was an obstacle in his path, and since he did not seem able to thrust a way through it he must find one round it, or over it, or under it.

He sat silently beside Lancaster in the car, his mind ranging over the possible suspects. Saunders appeared to be the only person connected with the case who could not have killed Maddison, for even if one took into account the possibility of Gillian lying to protect her husband the time factor cleared him completely. Gillian was seen cycling to the Fox at twenty minutes past six, and it could be safely assumed that she arrived not later than five minutes after being seen by the lorry driver. After that came the finding of her dying uncle, and the panicky ride to Ellwood House to her husband.

That left him with Major Oliver and Rhoda Maddison. If Rhoda murdered her brother it was going to be difficult to prove, since to all intents and purposes she was alone in the house, and there were no witnesses to say she was, or was not, in any particular place at any particular time. Added to which was the complete absence of physical clues which would respond to laboratory tests.

Major Oliver was the mystery element at the moment, with actions to his credit, or otherwise, whose purposes were not apparent. That he had queer connections with the Maddison family was obvious now, but the fact had crept up slowly on Knollis, so that he had not realised the truth of the matter until the poacher made his statement.

Maddison had lived in a house owned by Oliver. Oliver had lied to obtain for him the tenancy of the Fox. Oliver had been eager, if not desperate, to marry Rhoda Maddison. Oliver had spied on Maddison, and followed him some part of the way back to the inn. Why? Why was Oliver so curious regarding Maddison's midnight excursion?

"What's on your mind?" Lancaster asked at last, tired of the sphinx-like silence of his colleague.

"Oh, just thinking," said Knollis, shaking himself free of his reverie. He glanced round as they drove into the car-park of the inn. "We'll go into the saloon-bar. It will be cooler in there."

Lancaster grimaced, but made no comment.

"What are you drinking?" asked Knollis.

Lancaster stared at him. It was unlike Knollis to drink while on duty. "Er—drink? Well, a bottle of light ale, thanks."

Knollis rapped sharply on the counter, and Rhoda Maddison entered the bar, as prim and reserved as ever.

"Good morning, Miss Maddison. Two light ales, please," said Knollis, raising his hat. He took no further notice of her after receiving his change, but talked earnestly to Lancaster about the elements of the case which were now public property.

Suddenly he turned to Rhoda, who was polishing glasses at the end of the bar, and apparently not interested in their conversation.

"Oh, I almost forgot! We found these this morning, Miss Maddison. They seem to belong to you."

He slid the unsealed envelope along the counter. Rhoda Maddison met his casual manner with admirable unconcern, and put the envelope on a shelf under the counter as she thanked him.

Knollis turned back to Lancaster. "I was about to say, Lancaster, that we've gone about as far as we can, so I shall return to London tonight."

Lancaster put his glass on the counter. "You'll what? Go back to London? But hang it, man . . . !"

Knollis shrugged. "I can see no alternative."

"Packing in," grunted Lancaster. "I don't like folding up on a job."

"Neither do I," said Knollis. He drained his glass and pushed it forward. "Have another."

Lancaster slid his own glass across the counter. "I'm wondering what the Chief Constable's going to think about it!"

"Probably decide it's the only sensible move," replied Knollis.

Lancaster was frankly disgusted. He sipped his ale and eyed Knollis over the rim of the glass. It showed how wrong you could be in judging a man. He'd have been prepared to bet that Knollis would have stuck to a case until it fell to pieces in his hands.

"Shall we get back?" he asked ten minutes later. "I ought to ring the C.C."

Knollis hesitated, and pursed his lips. "No . . . o! That is, you go. I'll walk back over the top road, I want to be alone for a while, to think."

Lancaster brightened. "That's a different tone! By the time you get to town you'll have changed your mind!"

"Not me," Knollis assured him. "I'm leaving for home on the night train."

Lancaster snorted, and walked from the inn without another word. Knollis pushed forward his glass. "Another, Miss Maddison, please."

She eyed him curiously as she gently emptied the bottle into his glass. "Things not going well, Inspector? I couldn't help hearing what you said to Inspector Lancaster."

"I'm the only thing that's going well," he said jocularly. "I'm a pretty fair investigator, Miss Maddison, but I can't see through brick walls and oak doors."

"Brick walls—and oak doors?" she asked softly.

"I don't know what's behind your brother's death, Miss Maddison," said Knollis, "but all the evidence is concealed within the events of three nights—the night the talk arose about Captain Saunders' arrows, the night of your brother's murder, and the night you removed his papers to safe custody—there were others in the inn that night, of course."

"I've explained my parts in those events," she said in an even voice.

"I know you have," smiled Knollis, "but others have not!" He folded his arms and leaned on the bar counter.

"You see, Miss Maddison, a person who knows something about a murder *may* keep quiet for reasons in no way connected with the murder. If, say, a man engaged in breaking into a house for burglarious purposes comes across evidence of a murder, then, even though he may be able to clear himself of the murder charge, he will say nothing because of the possibility of receiving a long sentence for house-breaking."

Rhoda Maddison polished the same glass for the fourth time, rotating the glass-cloth inside it mechanically. "I see what you mean," she nodded.

"Those documents," said Knollis, jabbing a finger at the mahogany counter; "may I take it you've learned something from them? Something concerning your brother?"

She put the glass on the shelf behind her, and laid the cloth aside. She folded her hands, and stared blankly at him. "You're a shrewd man, Inspector Knollis!"

"I'm not so conceited as to believe that—not completely," Knollis replied with faint humour.

"My brother must have been something of a rogue," Rhoda Maddison mused.

"I've judged that."

"Since you've so kindly returned them to me it is obvious you've seen Major Oliver this morning."

Knollis gulped. He was glad she had not yet looked in the envelope and found some of its original contents missing. It was also nice to know that Oliver had not acquainted her with the loss of the whole batch.

"You'll know why I handed them to him," Rhoda said dreamily, staring through him. "I never believed my brother would descend to blackmail, and having complete confidence in Major Oliver—which I never had in my brother—I handed him the documents exactly as I found them, unsealed, so that he could remove whatever evidence my brother held against him."

Knollis raised his eyebrows into incredulous curves. "You mean you've no idea why your brother was blackmailing Major Oliver?"

"None, Inspector, and I never wish to know. I am going to marry Major Oliver now, and have no wish to pry into his past. Few people are without some skeleton in the cupboard, and having had a brother like Michael I am hardly in any position from which to judge others. We can start equal, and perhaps build a new life between us."

"I see," Knollis muttered, tracing a pattern in the spilt beer on the counter. He looked up. "Quite candidly, Miss Maddison, you have your own private ideas regarding the identity of your brother's killer?"

"I have," she admitted earnestly, "but while I find it difficult to condone the act I have to admit that—the person—the person had provocation. I could not have believed that a week ago, but circumstances tend to alter the trend of our thoughts."

She stared blandly at him for a few seconds, and then a slow smile came over the normally expressionless features.

"I think everything has happened for the best—even your decision to return to London."

"Thanks!" said Knollis with a twisted smile. He emptied his glass, raised his hat, said good morning, and left the inn, believing that Rhoda Maddison was convinced of Major Oliver's guilt.

He walked down Uppercroft Lane, and up Woodstock Lane to Oliver's house. The major was in his garden, spraying the roses against greenfly. He looked up and smiled a greeting as Knollis pushed open the gate and joined him beside the long border.

"Morning, Inspector! Want to see me, or just having a walk round?"

"I'd like a chat with you," said Knollis. He pulled the brim of his hat down to shade his eyes from the June sun, and regarded Oliver pensively. He was a fat and comfortable man, seemingly without a care in the world.

The major dropped the syringe in the bucket of insecticide, and wiped the wet left hand on the seat of his khaki gardening trousers.

"Come up to the house then, eh?"

Knollis walked with him, passing complimentary remarks about the roses in particular and the garden in general. They passed into a large entrance hall, where Knollis stared with amazement at the collection of souvenirs of the East spread across the walls.

"Quite a collection!" he commented.

Oliver nodded. "Not bad, eh? I was out East a deuce of a time, y'know, and the only way not to go mad is to have a hobby, so I collected native weapons and household implements."

"What are those two oval things?" Knollis asked as he indicated two almost black objects that looked like clumsy and irregular letters C. "I've never seen anything like them."

"Er—those?" asked Oliver. "Mongol yak-collars—like our English horse-collars, you know."

"Narrow in comparison with their length, aren't they?" suggested Knollis. "What will they be? Two feet six long and a foot or so wide?"

Oliver herrumphed. "Spring open, you know, and clamp on the driving poles. I must get them down to show you some time—but look, I must wash my hands, so suppose you make yourself at home in the sun-lounge. You'll find the cigarette-box. Won't keep you two minutes."

Knollis went to the lounge, and returned when Oliver was safely out of the way. He took out his notebook and pen and made a sketch of one of the alleged yak-collars. He was looking at the garden through an open window when Oliver returned.

"Now then," said Oliver, "what can I do for you?"

Knollis smiled on him. "You'll realise that we have to ask questions of anyone who was connected with Maddison? We have to get an all-round view of our man before we can get very far."

"Logical," said Oliver shortly.

"You knew him fairly well?"

"As a patron of the place, yes."

"Mind if I sit down?" Knollis asked.

Oliver bustled round to push a chair forward an inch. "My pardon, Inspector. Pre-occupied!"

"You insist that you knew Maddison only as the landlord of the Fox?" said Knollis. He leaned forward intently, his long fingers interlaced, and his forearms resting on his thighs.

Oliver glanced curiously at him, and repeated that he knew Maddison only as the landlord of the Fox Inn.

"Look, Major Oliver," said Knollis, "let's put the cards on the table, shall we? He lived in a house that belonged to you, in Surrey. You obtained the tenancy of the Fox for him. Yes, and Miss Maddison has acquainted me with certain facts this morning."

"Oh!" exclaimed Oliver. "She shouldn't have done that!"

"I'm afraid I gave her the impression that I had already had a chat with you," Knollis said easily. "You see, Major Oliver, I have to get my information somehow, and no one concerned with the case has been at all helpful up to now."

He fixed Oliver with keen grey eyes.

"You did know Maddison before he came to Teverby!"

"Yes," said Oliver. "Yes, I did, and I say it to my sorrow. He was a bad lot, you know!"

"I'm beginning to understand that," Knollis said in a dry tone.

Major Oliver ambled to the fireplace, stood on the oak curb, and rested his back against the white enamelled mantel. "I suppose you'll have to hear the thing," he sighed.

"It will save me the trouble of finding out for myself," said Knollis.

"The truth of the matter is that Maddison was in Military Intelligence during the last few years of his army career. He—well—he found information which he regarded as being to my discredit, and instead of doing his job he used the information to blackmail me. It was nothing, really," he said with a gesture, "but enough to damage my career, so I had to knuckle under."

"When did this begin?"

"Almost as soon as he got out of the service," grunted Oliver. "Life can be a bit confusing for a regular when his time is up. I was casting round for something to do with the rest of my life, and temporarily took on the management of an hotel in Guildford. I had a house outside Woking, and used to travel down by car every day. Maddison sought me out, and started by saying he wanted somewhere to live . . ."

He nodded heavily as he saw Knollis's brows lift.

"That's right, he took over my house and I had to live at the hotel. Truthfully, I was assisting with the management, and while wondering if the profession would suit me I was casting round for other possibilities. I wanted something permanent. Things looked grim for a time, and then the luck changed. I'd spent practically nothing during my years overseas, and bought shares in the company that owned the Fox—I had a friend on the board. I was offered a directorship, and took it. I bought this house and settled in, leaving Maddison to do as he liked in Surrey."

He grimaced. "Maddison wasn't content. He came to see me. Said he'd prefer to live nearer to me, and wouldn't mind a pub. That's how he got the Fox, of course."

"You gave the name of your house in Surrey as that of a pub once run by Maddison," said Knollis.

Oliver was surprised. "You know that? Well, it simplifies matters if you do, and saves further explanations."

"There's a personal, and perhaps impertinent, question, Major Oliver. You are dependent on your pension, your fees as director, and the income from your shares?"

"Oh yes! Entirely! I make no secret of that—but I'll have to find some odd job or other before long. Of course, if Miss Maddison's going to marry me we may keep the Fox in the family."

"All in all, you are somewhat relieved by Maddison's death?"

Oliver nodded slowly. "That must be the truth, mustn't it?"

"It's your own answer, Major Oliver, even if my question was a leading one. There's another matter I have to ask about. You told us about Maddison paying a call to Ellwood House . . ."

"True, I did."

"You didn't tell us you followed him back home."

Oliver jumped. "Wha—at?"

"You were followed in turn," Knollis explained. "You cut across the field to the elbow on Uppercroft Lane."

Oliver herrumphed again, and appeared to be embarrassed. "Followed? Who by, might I ask?"

"I can't tell you that, but I'd be grateful for an explanation."

"Er—well, I headed him off and demanded an explanation," Oliver stammered. "He had to walk up the hill from the corner of my lane, so I cut across the field. I wanted to know what the devil he was doing wandering round my place at midnight. He said he'd been to see Saunders, suspecting that Gillian might be there with him."

"And she wasn't?"

"She wasn't. Maddison had been bound to apologise to Saunders, and was on his way home, feeling humiliated."

Knollis rose, a whimsical smile on his lean features. "You know, Major Oliver, if only one of you people had gone to bed and stayed there this case would have been easier for me. You Teverby folk seem to be like owls, preferring the dark hours to the sunlit ones."

"It's deuced hot weather," complained Oliver. "Oh I know I've lived in the East, but that's different. It's the—"

"Humidity," said Knollis, cutting him short. He'd met people from the East before.

"Who else was out?" Oliver asked curiously.

"Isn't it sufficient to know that Captain Saunders and yourself both saw, and spoke to, Maddison after midnight? That Saunders reputedly rang Miss Maddison from Maunsby station at midnight—note that!—and that prior to that call Maddison was engaged in doing his accounts in the sitting-room of the inn? Weird, isn't it, when you put the facts against each other and check them."

He walked back to the village, found the local taxi owner, and chartered him to drive out to Brookdale to see Cowan, the bowyer and fletcher. "And keep quiet about where we are going!" he said.

Leonard Cowan was pleased to see him, and took him to his fletching shop at the rear of the premises. "We can swear here if we want to," he grinned. "Anyway, as one expert to another, how's the game going, Inspector?"

"Awkwardly," Knollis admitted. "It's full of contradictions."

"As uncertain as bow-making, eh?" said the red-haired bowyer. "You choose a billet of wood from a stock you've been seasoning for years, and you spend eight to twelve hours making the finest bow of your life; you test it, scrape a bit off here and a bit off there until the thing's nicely tillered, and then take it out to use it—and the thing splinters in your hand, and you have to get another billet of wood and start again. That the way your cases go, too?"

"Very often," said Knollis. "The main point is the starting again. You keep going until you've satisfied yourself and the customer—the law in this instance. Anyway, I've an idea in my head. Here's a sketch I've made. Can you tell me what it's supposed to be?"

Cowan took the notebook and considered the page careful before looking up with a quizzical expression on his face. "It *looks* like a Mongol bow! What's it supposed to be?"

"A horse-collar for a yak," Knollis told him with a grim smile.

"A toothbrush for my gear-box!" Cowan exclaimed. "A friend of mine has one of these efforts. They are native bows, made of horn, and backed with sinew."

"Colour?"

"Oh, like blackish old leather—brown leather that's considerably aged."

"That's it," Knollis nodded. "Must be difficult to pull, surely?"

Cowan threw back his head and laughed outright. "The thing's unstrung when it's like this. You have, literally, to turn it inside out, and then it looks like ye olde Cupid's bow as seen on valentines and wedding cakes! Heck of a job, too," he added more seriously. "Mongol bow, eh? I didn't think there were more than three in the county, and my friend Kesteven has one of them."

"And the other two . . ."

"Bloke at Teverby, queerly enough, Inspector—"

Cowan's jaw dropped, and he gazed at Knollis with shocked realisation. "Not *him*, surely!"

Then he thought for a moment, and said: "He's the only bloke round here who'd mention yaks."

"Any idea whether he can use 'em?" asked Knollis. "Is he an archer?"

Cowan wagged his red head. "Oh, he can! He can! We got him to give a display about three years ago when he first came this way. The club in this village was the first to be formed in the county, and we ran a demonstration to attract new members. Oliver gave us a demo with a moving target, using original Mongol arrows and a bow like that. Oh lord, yes, it must be him!"

He took a bow-string from the bench and wound it round his fingers. "That would explain one difficulty that's been bothering me since you came last time."

"Oh?"

"The difficulty of drawing a flat bow in that pub cellar. It could be done, but would be an awkward job if you were in a hurry—and I can't imagine Mr. Maddison parking himself against the board as a willing target. There's nobody in Teverby using a long bow, so we'll concentrate on flat bows. Now a flat bow should be the height of the archer, which means that when I'm drawing an arrow in a bow one half of the height or length of the bow is above my chin. I'm five feet nine. See the idea? I wouldn't exactly be roofing, but I wouldn't have any room for messing about. The Mongol bow is only just over three feet six when braced, and that would make all the difference. Y'see, it's a hunting bow . . ."

He dropped the string on the bench, and took up a red-dyed feather, with which he stroked his ear.

"There are short Western hunting bows, and short flight bows if it comes to that—for clout-shooting and flight-shooting and similar long-distance stunts, but none in the Teverby district, so it looks as if the Mongol bows—"

"But Captain Saunders told Inspector Lancaster that it was possible to draw a normal bow in the cellar," Knollis protested.

"It is," Cowan replied. "It's also possible to draw an umbrella in a fowl-shed—to open it, I mean."

Knollis was now sitting on Cowan's bench, his eyes narrowed to fine slits as he visualised the cellar of the Fox.

"Can I have your friend's address?" he asked. "I'd like to see his bow drawn and in action."

"Got a car?" asked Cowan.

"Came by taxi," Knollis replied laconically. "I paid it off."

"Then I'll take you over in my car if you like," said Cowan. "Kesteven's a school woodwork-master, and on his summer holiday."

"You can spare the time?"

"I can't, but I will do. I think I may be able to help you." Cowan talked archery all the time he was driving the eight miles to his friend's house, and it was evident to Knollis that the sport was his ruling passion.

"What about Robin Hood's famous shooting?" Knollis asked when he could get a word in.

Cowan gave a dry laugh. "Highly exaggerated. Either that, or we've lost the true skill of the game. Ever heard of Roger Ascham? He was Queen Elizabeth's tutor when her father was on the throne, and he wrote the book called *Toxophilus*—probably the first treatise ever written on archery. He said everything then known about archery, and yet he never mentions such tricks as wand-splitting and so on. No, I think the old ballad-writers hotted up the yarns for popular consumption. Still, that isn't the be-all and end-all of archery. It's a fine sport for getting you out into the open air, and exercising every muscle of your body. You should take it up!"

"It isn't many months since a man tried to persuade me to keep bees," Knollis said dryly, "and a few days later I was in hospital, stung to blazes, and having adrenalin pumped into me."

Cowan laughed. "Oh well, this is different! The worst you can do with a bow is—"

"Murder," said Knollis.

Cowan put his head back to laugh loudly, and then dragged the car back from the grass verge of the country lane down which they were careering.

"That's Kesteven's place, the cottage on the right. Best little bowyer in the country. He taught me to make 'em, and still whacks me hollow. You'll like him."

Kesteven was a bespectacled little man with dark hair and a ready smile. A motor-cycle stood against a long wooden workshop behind the house, and at the far end of the garden hung an archery target, its gold centre, circled by red, blue, black, and white rings glaring brightly in the June sunshine.

"Scotland Yard come to pick you up at last, Charlie," said Cowan. "Inspector Knollis, investigating the Maddison affair. He wants you to show him how to brace and draw the old body-belt. Somebody's been giving him an idea."

Without asking questions Kesteven went into his workshop and came out with the Mongol bow.

"That's similar," said Knollis keenly.

"He's seen one," Cowan said with a significant nod of his red head.

Kesteven squinted over his glasses. "Putting two and two together I can have three guesses and one to spare, and know why you want to see this drawn, and who you're thinking about," he said.

"We must ignore guesses," replied Knollis with a smile. "I can't afford to guess on my job."

"Who can?" queried Kesteven.

He slipped the loop of the bowstring over the upper tip of the bow, and then performed a series of acrobatics accompanied by grunts. He was nearly on his knees in the end, but got to his feet with a triumphant "A-ah!"

"That," said Cowan, "is it."

"Interesting," said Knollis, examining the bow.

"Good job you didn't come yesterday," said Kesteven. "It's been out on loan for demonstration purposes. Anyway, this is how you use it. Get me those old arrows from the back of the shed, Len. Now, Inspector, you push the pile—the point—between the string and the bow, and then draw the nock—the feathered end—back to the string, fitting the nock—the nick in the end—to the string where this green silk is bound round it. When drawing, you don't hold the bow out at arm's length and pull the string back, but bring bow and string up together, drawing them equally. That's to save muscular energy. See my fingers? I'm using what we call the Mediterranean loose, two fingers hooked on the string below the arrow, and one above, both clear of the arrow itself. See how I've got my right hand anchored on my jaw-bone? Now I loose the string—see?"

There was a sharp twang, and the arrow fled the length of the garden toward the target.

"I can't see it now," said Knollis.

"You won't," said Cowan. "It's gone right through. There's nearly sixty pounds behind that arrow when it leaves this bow. Now that's the point, because it was an ordinary wooden target arrow with a bullet nose. The arrows used in the Fox cellar were metal, with spear and bodkin piles. All that tell you anything, Inspector?"

"The distance down your garden, Mr. Kesteven?"

"Just twenty-five yards from where we stand."

"Yes," said Knollis, answering Cowan's question. "It tells me a great deal, thanks, but I'm trying to weigh up the effect of this bow, with metal arrows, at a shorter distance."

Kesteven scratched his head. "Well, during the war, when the Duke decided to reduce his herd of deer, he let me shoot a few of them for him . . ."

"Results first time, and no questions asked by the deer," Cowan interrupted.

"Distance?" asked Knollis.

"Oh, about the same distance as here—twenty-five yards."

"How far did the arrows penetrate?"

"Over halfway, using wooden shafts with steel piles. The alloy ones Len is making would probably go in up to the flights."

"You used this bow?"

"No, a forty-eight pound flat bow."

"Want to know anything else?" asked Cowan, with the air of a salesman who still had plenty of bargains up his sleeve.

"Where's the nearest station where I can catch the earliest train to London," said Knollis.

"I can run you two miles to Woodholme station," replied Cowan. "You should catch the Leeds-St. Pancras express with half an hour to spare."

"You won't mind doing that?"

"I told you I'd help in any way possible."

"Would you mind ringing Inspector Lancaster when you get home," said Knollis, "and tell him I'll be back in forty-eight hours. It might set his mind at rest. He thinks I've packed in the case."

Cowan chuckled. "He evidently doesn't know his man!"

Chapter XIV
THE EXPOSING OF MAJOR OLIVER

Gordon Knollis reported to his superiors at the Yard early the next morning, and then took a walk down the Embankment. Here, remote from Teverby, it was possible to see the Maddison case more objectively. There, he had been one of the actors in the play. Here, he could sit in the gallery, as it were, and look down on the stage. A murder case was a play never finished until the culprit had been apprehended, tried, found guilty, and sentenced, and he was necessarily a character in the presentation, a character in conflict with most of the others taking part. It was Knollis and Company versus The Others, especially if The Others were in sympathy with the murderer, as they seemed to be in this instance. All of them had been relieved, if not actually pleased, to see Michael Maddison depart this life, even though he departed violently, and it was evident that while the innocent parties didn't intend seeing themselves arraigned in a court of law on the capital charge they were not going to assist in helping the culprit into the dock.

All of them had good reasons for wishing Maddison out of the way. Rhoda Maddison was needing her freedom, as well as the money which was her rightful inheritance. Gillian, so passionately devoted to Saunders that she had married him against her uncle's orders, was anxious to avoid the mysterious consequences with which he had threatened her. Saunders, similarly threatened, had a similar motive. Oliver needed relief from Maddison's blackmailing operations. Four people with sound motives, all apparently capable of handling a bow, all apparently with means of access to the Fox and its cellar, and all with either nice tight little alibis or without a shred of evidence against them. It was some case!

Saunders was covered by his wife's evidence. Oliver was never seen nearer to the Fox than the elbow of Uppercroft Lane. Rhoda was in bed, sleeping soundly after a late night. Gillian found her uncle dying in the cellar. It was all as simple as that, and yet it was evident to Knollis that there was a twist somewhere in the case. Someone was lying, or there was collusion, or, worse, he had missed some vital point of evidence, had failed to give some item the significance which it deserved, a matter for which, if he ever discovered it, he would never forgive himself.

Comparing the motives, it seemed that Major Oliver's was the strongest of the four. Here was a man, known and respected in his neighbourhood, who was being milked of his income, a man well beyond middle age who needed such money as he had to finance the autumn and winter of his life. The blackmailer never knew when to stop, never took into account that the goose could only lay so many golden eggs in its lifetime. Oliver was probably approaching the point where he would see his lifetime's savings vanish completely unless he did *something*. Despite the fact that the police protected the identity of a blackmailed person it was all too seldom that such a person was prepared to expose himself even to them. Instead, he took the law into his own hands, and it looked as if this was what Oliver had done. It only looked as if this was what he had done; there was not a single shred of proof. The thing to be done at the moment was the establishing of Oliver's motive. Knollis was always of the belief that his colleagues knew the trend of this thoughts, and he now hoped that Lancaster was spending his time checking the major's movements. For the rest, he had given Rhoda Maddison the idea that the case was closed, and there was a chance that when this news had got round someone concerned with the case would make a slip.

Knollis walked a hundred yards beyond Cleopatra's Needle and then turned and walked back to the Yard at a brisk pace. He saw Superintendent Burnell, and made several requests, and then left the Yard and took a train to Woking. He was in the town until shortly after noon, asking questions of people who had known both Oliver and Maddison. Then he found a Guildford-bound bus and went to see the manager of the hotel at which Oliver had worked for a time. He returned to his home in North London that night, and early next morning went to see the firm of solicitors who had dealt with the affairs of Gillian Maddison's father. He got back to the Yard at half-past eleven, and saw Burnell once more before having a lengthy talk with Lancaster over the 'phone. His afternoon was devoted to interviews with mysterious people connected with M.I.5, and early in the evening he caught a train back to Maunsby.

Lancaster was waiting with his car.

"Well?" Lancaster asked with more hope than expectancy as Knollis tumbled into the seat beside him.

"It's coming now," said Knollis. "We'll take the minor details first. You'll remember Maddison made veiled threats to Gillian, threatening something or other if she married Saunders—or anyone else? His guardianship ended on her twenty-first birthday, but he was still trustee for the estate, and while that trusteeship ended on her wedding day, Maddison had to approve her choice of a husband. If he didn't, he still administered the estate—meaning that no husband of Gillian's could get a cent of her money. Maddison was then obviously threatening her with penury, unless her husband was in a position to support her. A somewhat similar state of affairs existed with regard to Rhoda Maddison. Maddison supplied her with money, *at his own discretion*, until she married, but that clause means that even if she'd discovered the true state of affairs while he was alive she couldn't have done anything about it. Well, she could, but how could she force a legal argument when she hadn't the money to finance it?"

"So her only hope of getting her money was—well, by Michael Maddison dying!" exclaimed Lancaster.

"That's it!" said Knollis. "Pretty, isn't it?"

"And what else, Knollis?"

"Sit back for a shock, and don't let go the wheel," said Knollis. "I got the Super to pull a few strings and managed to get the dope on Oliver and Maddison and their service careers."

Lancaster raised his eyes from the road. "You don't mean M.I.5 came clean about Maddison?"

"They'd never heard of him, Lancaster."

"What? But Oliver told us . . . !"

"On the other hand the War Office told me a lot about Maddison, and the Military Intelligence branch told me a lot about Oliver!"

Lancaster digested those facts, and was still thinking them over as he pulled into the kerb outside police headquarters. He braked, and then turned to Knollis with an incredulous expression on his face.

"You mean the roles were reversed? That it was Oliver who was M.I.5, and Maddison only the soldier?"

Knollis nodded.

"But that means . . ."

Knollis nodded again. "Don't your investigations prove it?" he asked anxiously.

Lancaster grimaced. "Maddison had hardly a bean to his name, and Oliver's been shoving money in the bank, and buying shares, and having a whale of a time."

"Proving that it was *Oliver* who was blackmailing *Maddison*."

"Yes," said Lancaster. "Yes."

Knollis leaned back in his seat and closed his eyes.

"There's a thing two branches of the War Office would like to prove, and they can't. You see, Lancaster, both Maddison and Oliver were messing about in Burma, and India generally, at the same time. Maddison was apparently engaged in collecting material for a book on Asiatic political economy, and consequently mixing with all and sundry. Now it came about that a leak occurred, and Major Oliver was called on to investigate it. It was at the time when we were preparing to pull out of India, and a delicate state of affairs existed. Oliver eventually reported that he couldn't get the proof he needed, but he knew his man. It was Maddison."

Lancaster sniffed.

"Maddison's flair for mixing with all and sundry was well known, and while no proof was forthcoming it was felt that Oliver was right, so Maddison was posted home, and offered the opportunity of resigning his commission. He'd no alternative but to take it."

"Yes," said Lancaster.

"Now certain people in London weren't too sure about Oliver, whose finances were in a more than satisfactory state considering his position," went on Knollis. "When Maddison was out of the country, and the thing had died down, Oliver was also posted home—"

"And given the opportunity of resigning," said Lancaster. "Yes, I see the thing clearly."

"The argument put to me in London was this," said Knollis; "that Oliver must know that they are still on the job, and waiting, and that the odds are in favour of them getting him one day—"

"When he'll either be shot, or shoved in for life," interrupted Lancaster.

"So that, knowing this, Oliver is feathering—well, not his nest, but at least a few cabin trunks, and then one day he'll catch a little boat at Tilbury, and finish up—"

"In the Argentine, or Brazil."

"That's it," said Knollis.

"And this forthcoming marriage with Rhoda Maddison?"

"Surely another stage in the process of gathering riches unto himself ready for his getaway."

"Hm!" said Lancaster, scratching his ear.

"Hm—what?" asked Knollis.

"If he did bump off Maddison, I'm wondering why it all happened—the house at Woking—the tenancy of the Fox—and eventually the murdering of Maddison."

"So far as the house at Woking is concerned, as with the tenancy of the Fox," said Knollis, "the answer obviously is that Oliver wanted him right under his eye, wanted to be able to see what he was doing. Oh yes, and there's another point. Neither Rhoda nor Gillian Maddison seemed to know what Michael was doing with his time when in Surrey. He was answering Sits. Vacant, trying to find himself a job. He got one, and then suddenly turned it down, saying that domestic matters necessitated his removal to the Midlands."

"Oliver forced him to the Fox!"

"Seems that way," Knollis said with a sigh. "So far as your query regarding Oliver's motive is concerned, the answer is—I don't know!"

"The kitty wasn't exhausted, was it?" Lancaster asked hopefully.

"Not by any manner of means. Both Rhoda and Gillian Maddison have nice handlings waiting for them."

"Maddison got the real gen on the India job, and had turned it on Oliver?"

"No proof of it," said Knollis. "I thought about that, and asked about it, and the answer seemed to be that Maddison was in the worst possible position to follow up the business, and would certainly be the last to hear if his name was cleared—their point being that they were more interested in convicting Oliver, which would automatically clear Maddison's name. And as even Maddison wasn't told of his alleged peccadillo—see what I mean?"

"On the face of it I'd say Oliver had worked a first-class bluff across Maddison," said Knollis. "I think he must have told Maddison why he was turfed out, and concocted a pile of false clues which Maddison could neither prove nor disprove. The bloke was in a cleft-stick. It only needed Oliver to start talking in the wrong place, and Maddison, innocent or guilty, was finished in the licensing business. Then he only needed to extend the grapevine, and Maddison would find himself unsuitable for every job for which he applied. It was Oliver, not Maddison, who was the rat. Maddison was only a small mouse in comparison."

"So we have to turn all our dogs on Oliver," said Lancaster. "We have to think out how he got to the Fox that morning without being seen, and how he got back again ditto."

"If he was in the wine store," said Knollis, "he could have followed Gillian down the lane. She wouldn't have seen him, for she was in too much of a darned hurry to make sure her hubby was at home. Once he got within sight of his house, and away from the Fox, he was just a retired gentleman taking an early morning walk, it being too hot to sleep—the humidity and all that."

"It still is," said Lancaster. "What about a run out into the country, and talk as we go? We've got to map out some plan of campaign, and we can do it as well out there as in my office, which is like an oven in spite of the fans."

Knollis agreeing, Lancaster started the car and ran it from the close air of the town. He took the western road, over the hill and down into Teverby. At the Fox he turned to the right, and was changing down to take the hill outside the Wain when the Teverby constable stepped from behind one of the buttresses.

Lancaster pulled up. "It's us, looking for fresh air," he said with a smile.

The constable saluted. "Not a bad night, sir. I'd hate to be in Maunsby tonight!"

"The air's as thick as treacle," said Lancaster. "You can feel it sticking to you. Everything okay round here?"

"Nice and quiet, sir. You got the message I sent in an hour ago?"

"No," said Lancaster, "I haven't been back since I met Inspector Knollis off the London train. What's it in aid of?"

"Nothing important, I don't suppose, sir, but a chap who lives above me saw a bike outside the Fox at twenty past six that morning when Mr. Maddison was found."

"That'd be Miss Gillian's," said Lancaster.

"It would not," said Knollis. "She was at the top of the hill at twenty past."

Lancaster turned to glance at him. "Yes, that's right. She was. Twenty past, eh? Now what does that mean?"

"The man in the wine cellar had to come on something, either his feet or a bike," said Knollis.

"Then," demanded Lancaster, "if he was still in the cellar—on the premises—when she arrived, why didn't she see him?"

"Excuse me, sirs," said the constable.

"What is it?" Knollis asked, and then opened the door of the car and got out.

"Well, sir, the Fox isn't a square building. It has a long frontage that takes in the smoke-room, the side lobby, the saloon bar, and the off-sales department. The house narrows twice as it gets to the back. The second section, as you might call it, has a room less on each end, and then right at the back you've a bit with only the kitchen, the scullery, and the pantry in it. Seen in plan it looks like a pedestal with three steps. If the bike was in one of the returns, as the builders call 'em, the bike perhaps couldn't be seen from the angle at which Miss Gillian approached it."

"That's a point, you know," said Lancaster, who had now joined them in the middle of the lane. "We must check on that."

"And that reminds me that I've a point," said the constable, glancing at his watch. "Ten past twelve, and I have to ring the station from the call-box at the top."

He saluted, and walked off.

Lancaster was about to pass some remark to Knollis when he saw his back was turned, and he was staring intently through the half-light toward Major Oliver's house.

"Now what is it?" he asked testily.

"There's a light on," said Knollis.

"The old boy seems to spend most of his time out of bed," snorted Lancaster. "There's nothing unusual in seeing a light burning."

"There's an idea in my head," said Knollis. "You know, Lancaster, I never did believe that he never went further than the top of this lane when he cut across the field to intercept Maddison. And that's another thing which solves itself. I wondered at the time how he came to be in a position to demand of Maddison where he had been and why. Now we know he was the blackmailer it is clear. I suggest we turn the car up Woodstock Lane, and then decide on the spur of the moment to look in on him. It's far too hot to sleep, isn't it?"

"As you say," said Lancaster. He got back into the car.

Major Oliver was leaning on the gates at the foot of his drive.

Lancaster drove a few yards past, and then pulled up as if on a second thought.

Knollis leaned from the car. "Someone else can't sleep, Major?"

Oliver opened the gate and came to stand beside the car. "Wondered who it was. Saw the lights outside the Wain, y'know!"

"Just having a run round to cool off, and dropped across the constable," said Lancaster easily. "Now we're hopping off home to see if it's cooled off enough for us to attempt sleep. Marvellous word, cool. It makes me feel more comfortable to keep saying it."

"Anything new?" asked Oliver. "I shouldn't ask you that, I suppose, but you know what curiosity is!"

"We've nothing to tell you yet," Knollis said ambiguously. Then he smiled. "We could ask you a few questions, of course, just to keep the party alive!"

"Questions?" grunted Oliver. "Don't know that I seem good at answering them, do I? They don't seem to have helped you up to now."

"There's one which might do," said Knollis. "You remember the night when you cut across this field opposite your house to have a word with Maddison?"

"Of course, yes!"

"At what time did you leave the Fox?"

"Leave the Fox? Leave the—"

Oliver stared at Knollis, and lowered his eyes, meanwhile scraping the toe of his leather slipper round an arc of the wing.

"I didn't go to the Fox," he said shortly.

"Didn't you, Major Oliver? Didn't you really?" Knollis asked in a mock-coaxing voice. "You're absolutely sure about that?"

Oliver looked up, almost defiantly. "Didn't expect me to volunteer the information, considering the circumstances, did you?"

"Someone else had the same excuse, but we cleared them of all suspicion as a result of the admission," said Knollis.

"Oh, Well. Well, yes, it would be just after one o'clock. Perhaps a bit later. Might have been half-past. I don't know."

The major grumbled truculently.

"You know, you fellows expect everybody to go round looking at their watches and making notes in a diary. People don't live like that! They—they—well, they go about their business, and—well, that's it!"

"We're only too painfully aware of it," said Knollis. "Er—was your business so private that you couldn't discuss it in an empty lane at something after midnight?"

"It was private business—and nothing to do with what happened later."

"That's reassuring to hear," said Knollis.

"It was about his sister, if you want to know!"

"I don't," said Knollis.

"I'd twice asked her to marry me, and she said there were reasons why she couldn't, so I boned Maddison about it, and wanted to know if he considered the reasons . . ."

"Yes?"

"He told me to mind my own business and he'd mind his, and then told me to get to blazes out of it. He wanted to get on with his books."

"He saw you off the premises?"

"No, I let myself out—by the side door there's been so much fuss about."

"You didn't notice anything unusual about the latch when you closed the door, Major Oliver?"

"There again," snorted Oliver, "you expect peaceful people like myself to live in a melodramatic world—going round checking my times and dates, listening for latches that don't click when they should. Hell's curry, man, my head was filled with something else!"

"Than hell's curry," said Knollis. "I quite understand."

The major stood staring at him, his face red and his eyes wide with annoyance.

"You'd be relieved when you knew Captain Saunders had married Miss Gillian?" Knollis suggested.

"Too much of a charmer, that man," said Oliver. "No depth to him, y'know. A materialist of the worst kind. No control over his thoughts or his emotions!"

"Like you?"

"Like me," the major repeated. "A woman wants a steady rock on which she can lean in times of stress—"

"A solid rock shouldn't allow storms and times of stress to arise, surely," murmured Knollis.

"Man always has to face circumstance and struggle with it," went on the major. "The materialist who is in conflict with the dramatic situations of life has no anchor, no spiritual harbour! He is out in the open sea, tossed and thrown about by the winds of fortune!"

"I'm going to burst into tears any moment," said Knollis, "but apart from that, aren't we getting away from the point?"

"I was saying that Saunders has no control over his emotions, and a fluffy-headed slip of a girl like Gillian is suitable for him. Now myself and Miss Maddison—"

He almost beamed in the half-light.

"Are temperamentally suited?" suggested Knollis.

"That's it, old man. She was inclined to be taken in by his suave charm, but she learned his worth when he slunk off and married her niece in some dingy back street—probably in a registry office."

"In a church at Eastness," said Knollis.

"The same thing, isn't it?" demanded Oliver. "They didn't get married here, in their own village, did they?"

"I see what you mean," Knollis said quietly. "We can take it that you were glad when she was—er—free of the charms of the two-faced serpent who slithered into the house and made love to both girls at once—if you'll forgive me losing control over my emotions and slipping into melodramatic speech!"

"Quite all right, old man!" Oliver said magnanimously. "And now I must go and complete my inhalations of the divine prana, and then to bed for an hour or so."

Lancaster started the engine and slipped the clutch. "And we'll inhale the divine bouquet of the dew of the glens, and do likewise," he said.

Knollis was at Ellwood House shortly after nine the next morning, with Lancaster striding along behind him and wondering what queer bee he had in his bonnet this time. It was like working with a ventriloquist's dummy which had lost its master, and consequently its power of speech.

Saunders was lounging round the house in his pyjamas and a green silk dressing gown, a cigarette hanging from the corner of his mouth.

"Early to bed, and late to rise is a wonderful way of life," he commented as he met them at the door. "Do come in!"

"Wife not about?" asked Knollis.

Saunders gestured toward the ceiling. "Messing about in her boudoir, probably adding war-paint to her undeniably attractive features. Women are like that, you know! Want to see her?"

"No, we want to see you without her being present," said Knollis. "Maddison called round here at midnight—midnight before the morning he was killed."

Saunders nodded coolly. "Sounds as if my friend has been busy again. Yes, Maddison did make a call. He wondered if Gillian was here, and she wasn't, as you know!"

"What made him suspicious?"

"Can't you guess?" asked Saunders.

"We don't guess. We can't afford to do it," said Knollis. "You don't seem surprised to hear that we know about his visit!"

"Let's be frank, shall we?" said Saunders. "I am a democrat, and make friends with all kinds and conditions of men. There's a certain little man who is attracted to an innocent but illegal occupation known as poaching. Right! He tells me that Oliver watched Maddison come to my house, and then the said Oliver followed Maddison back at least as far as the corner of Upper-croft Lane. Now ask yourself who peached on Gillian and I?"

"Major Oliver?"

Saunders nodded. "He's a rat if ever there was one. I knew all along that he wanted Rhoda, and as I didn't I put him wise to the elopement, asking him to use his discretion and not to comment to anyone if there was too much dashing to and fro of cars on the night when we came back from Eastness. You see, I had the whole thing planned out. I meant bringing the girls back for a drink, and then taking them home to the Denby place at Maunsby, and ringing Rhoda from the call-box and everything. I thought Oliver would be relieved to know I was completely out of the running."

"And he peached on you?"

Saunders stuck his tongue under his lip, and shrugged. "Serves me right. You shouldn't trust anyone but yourself."

"Why did he tell Maddison?"

"Dunno, Inspector, unless the old fool was smitten with burning passion and wanted to clarify the position in the hope that Maddison would say, Oh Well, and So What! Candidly, I don't get it at all—except that I've found he isn't to be trusted any more."

"A question in confidence," said Knollis. "You've been in his house, and seen the souvenirs in his entrance hall? What are those two things he told me were horse-collars for yaks? Black-ish-brown and leathery things, like crumpled letters C?"

Saunders looked stolidly at him for a full minute while he crushed the remains of his cigarette deep into an ash-tray.

"So you're wise to him, eh? If you are talking about what I think you are, you're referring to two Mongol bows, relics he brought back with him."

"Any idea whether they'll work?"

Saunders laughed. "They'll work all right! Capable of—well, killing a man in a cellar!"

"Can Oliver use them?"

Saunders looked at them from under his brows, significantly. "He can use them! I've seen him use them! He can hit things, too."

"How could—a person—carry them, say, from your archery field to the Fox without them being too noticeable?"

"I'm no detective, but I have thought about this business," Saunders said reflectively, "and I know how I'd have done it."

"Well?" asked Knollis. He was standing erect, his back like a ram-rod as he faced the man who was almost his double.

Saunders broke into a smile. "I'd have tied the ruddy thing to the frame of a bike, hung my jacket over the bar, and biked it to the Fox. A lady's bike would be excellent for the job."

"Has he a lady's cycle?" asked Lancaster.

"He has two girls working there who both live in the village, and I know one of them had a puncture the night before, and walked home, leaving Johnson—Oliver's man—to mend it the next morning."

"You're surprisingly helpful," Knollis said suspiciously.

"I don't think I've anything to thank Oliver for, and I don't owe him anything," said Saunders. "I've merely answered your questions like a good witness, and I haven't for one moment suggested that my neighbour, Major Oliver, murdered Gillian's uncle."

"True," said Knollis. "All you've done is hand us the rope with the noose already made in one end."

"What you do with it is your own affair," said Saunders.

CHAPTER XV
THE DISAPPOINTMENT OF KNOLLIS

KNOLLIS AND LANCASTER went straight on to Woodstock House to interview Major Oliver once more, and Oliver made no attempt to disguise the fact that he was sick of seeing them.

"Can't you ask all your questions at one go?" he demanded testily. "I keep a roller for use on the drive, and it's more efficient than the feet of policemen."

"Sorry, really," Knollis said in a soothing voice. "It does happen like this, you know, and we can do little about it. There's a point, Major Oliver—"

"There always is when you appear," said Oliver. "When you've done with the point, you say you have just one final question, and after that we get a dozen or so supplementary questions."

"That's right," Knollis said with remarkable candour. "We don't always find witnesses as intelligent as yourself, and consequently we're inclined to lump 'em together into one class. As it happens, there is only one question this time—and perhaps a few supplementary questions."

"Oh well," said the major, somewhat mollified. He threw his secateurs on the grass, removed the left-hand glove he was wearing, and squatted on his haunches.

"There's a local poacher by the name of Wilson," said Knollis non-committally.

"I know the rascal," said the major with a grin. "He may be agin the law, but I have to admire his skill. He's a wizard with game!"

"Why did you tell the local constable that Wilson was working Burnaby Wood on the night before Maddison's death?"

Oliver got to his feet, and stood for a second with his hands on his plump hips. "Oh, that!"

"That!" said Knollis.

"Er—well, I don't know whether I can tell you. It concerns another man—Saunders, as a matter of fact."

"You knew Saunders and Miss Gillian Maddison were making a runaway marriage, of course!"

Major Oliver's huge red features cleared. "Oh well, if you know that it's different. Saunders took me into his confidence because he said there would be a deal of car-running up and down the lane on the night they came home from their honeymoon, and he asked me not to comment on it in the village because of Maddison getting to know. He knew I was interested in Miss Rhoda, of course, and it was, in a way, a family matter."

"Yes, but how does this affect the yarn the bobby had from you—or perhaps I should say how did the yarn affect Saunders?"

Oliver smiled slowly. "The fewer people who knew the better. That's how I looked at it. Robinson patrols part of this lane, and I thought he'd be better out of the way."

"Was Wilson to work Burnaby Wood?"

"Not so far as I know," grinned Oliver. "He had occasional drinks at my expense, and sometimes told me of his exploits, but he didn't take me into his confidence regarding future plans—naturally."

"And it was with this in mind that you followed Maddison that night?"

"Oh yes, of course. It seemed to me he'd got a hint of what had happened, and I wanted to know if possible, because if he had, then I didn't want Saunders to think I'd split on him."

"I see," Knollis said dryly, remembering what Saunders had told them not so many minutes earlier. He turned abruptly with a short word of thanks and marched to the gates and the car, Lancaster scratching his head and following him tamely, a puzzled man.

"Why the deuce didn't you keep at him?" he demanded as he turned the car in the narrow lane.

"I was going to do so," said Knollis, "and then remembered that if we weren't careful we were going to step on the toes of the M.I.5 people—and that's something we mustn't do!"

"You know what we're going to finish up with?" Lancaster asked moodily.

"Circumstantial evidence, and an unsatisfactory case to take into court," said Knollis. "I know it, my friend, and it is worrying me."

"Well, what do we do now?" said Lancaster.

"Wait until we can get Oliver's man alone in the house. You'd better put a few shadows on to let us know when he goes out, and to where he goes. Meanwhile we'll have another chat with Rhoda Maddison. You hop into the call-box while I park the car for you."

The church clock was striking eleven, and Rhoda Maddison opening the main door of the inn as they approached. She beckoned them to use the lobby entrance, met them there, and took them to the private sitting-room. Without asking them, or indeed saying a word, she poured out two liberal glasses of whisky and splashed them lightly with soda. She filled herself a glass with sherry and held it up. "Cheerio!" She seated herself on the arm of the settee, and looked at each of them in turn. "As you say you are closing the case, I wonder if you'd tell me exactly what did take place in my house that morning—so far as you are aware."

"The story's straightforward, Miss Maddison," Knollis said with apparent frankness. "It's the proof that has beaten us. Your brother seems to have risen at the usual hour and gone down the cellar for his morning secret archery practice. While he was there his murderer crept into the house by the side door, went down the cellar, and shot two arrows at him. One missed, and the other took him through the chest.

"Your niece seems to have been suspicious of her husband, and believed that he had made her stay the night in Maunsby, not because he was afraid of her uncle learning the truth regarding their marriage, but because he intended murdering him. She borrowed her friend's cycle, and came from Maunsby to try to prevent the crime. She found her uncle dying in the cellar, unable to speak because of his injuries, and bolted to her husband. She says," he added slowly, "that someone was hidden in the wine and spirit cellar."

"That's correct," Rhoda Maddison said slowly. "Someone had broached a bottle of whisky."

Knollis blinked. "What!"

"Why didn't you tell us that?" shouted Lancaster. "Where is the bottle now?"

"I decanted the whisky and threw the bottle away. You see, the person in the cellar had knocked the neck from the bottle."

"But the bottle!" said Lancaster frantically.

"I threw it in the dustbin, of course."

"Has the dustbin been emptied?" Knollis asked.

Rhoda Maddison stroked her forehead. "See, they come on Wednesdays. Yes, it will have been emptied twice by now."

"Oh, my God!" exclaimed Lancaster. "You carry on here, Knollis. I'll see to it!"

He vanished through the doorway, and a few seconds later his car was heard speeding up the hill toward Maunsby.

"You've been remarkably helpful all the way through this affair," said Knollis caustically. An idea occurred to him, and he stared keenly at the mistress of the Fox Inn.

"What—what is it?" she stammered, momentarily shaken from her usual calm by the intensity of Knollis's expression.

"Then you didn't sleep through until Miss Cromwell aroused you at something after nine o'clock," he said. "No one was allowed into the wine store until Inspector Lancaster arrived from Maunsby, and he didn't—most certainly didn't—find a broken bottle there, or he would have taken it away, and mentioned it in your report. You were downstairs, and in the cellar long before nine o'clock, Miss Maddison!"

He walked slowly after her as she rose and backed toward the wall of the room.

"You not only knew that your brother was dead when Miss Cromwell awoke you, but you had seen him lying there on the floor of the cellar! It couldn't have been you who took Captain Saunders' hunting arrows from the bar that night, could it? It couldn't have been you who hid them in the golf bag in the lobby? It couldn't have been you, who, knowing your brother's regular morning routine, followed him down the cellar and shot him to death? It couldn't have been you who fastened yourself in the wine cellar and hid while your niece came running down the steps, found her uncle, and raced away in her panic? Could it, Miss Maddison? Could it?"

She pressed herself into the wall, her clasped fingers tight against her throat and her lips parted.

"Could it?" persisted Knollis. "Could it, Miss Maddison!"

"I—I didn't kill him," she whispered. "It was I who hid in the wine store. I heard a noise, and got up, and came down . . ."

"Why did you get up when you heard the noise?" asked Knollis. "At what time did you get up, Miss Maddison?"

"It was twenty past six," she said in a low voice.

"Why should you get up at twenty minutes past six just because you heard a noise?" asked Knollis, his features tense, his eyes like slits. "Didn't both yourself and your niece agree in the presence of Inspector Lancaster and myself that your brother Michael was a born banger-about? Didn't Miss Gillian say he couldn't move quietly if he tried? Between yourself and the cellar was a long corridor carpeted thickly, and the thickly carpeted stairs, and the terrazzo floor of the lobby, and the cellar steps. Was it such a loud noise, Miss Maddison? Did the murderer fire the arrows from a gun? Nonsense!"

He paused, his hands plunged deep into the pockets of his discreet grey jacket, his head pushed forward on his shoulders.

In a quiet voice he asked: "Tell me, Miss Maddison, why you really left your bed and went down to the cellar at twenty minutes past six? Could it be that more people than one had planned and plotted Michael Maddison's death? Could that be possible, Miss Maddison? Perhaps you intended to bring about his death yourself, or perhaps you and one other had conspired to kill him. Is there any other reason why you should have gone to the cellar?"

She pressed her back hard to the wall, obviously straining and striving to gain control over herself.

"There can be no other explanation, Miss Maddison," Knollis went on. "Either you went to kill him, or you went to meet someone who intended to kill him."

Rhoda Maddison's arms fell to her sides. She raised her chin defiantly, her features set like a carved statue. Below the sleekly brushed-back hair a tiny vein throbbed in her temple, blue against the whiteness of the skin.

"I went to kill him," she said.

"Ah!" said Knollis, and all the tenseness left him in one second.

"I went to kill him," said Rhoda Maddison again. "I will tell you everything for the first and the last time. You have no witnesses, and even if you put me in court with a Testament in my hand I will swear my soul away rather than repeat it."

Her long fingers stroked the black silk dress smoothly over her thighs, and came to rest before her, the fingers interlaced in the manner so characteristic of her.

"I'd had enough of Michael," she said. "I'd borne with him for years, far too many years. He had charge of my money, and let me have but little of it. He ignored me as if I was his servant. Then he forbade me to marry, and that was the last straw. I knew there was only one way out. I had to kill my brother Michael."

Knollis waited for her, anxious not to break the train of her thoughts.

"Once I had made up my mind," she said icily, "I began to watch him. He thought I was brainless, but I knew what he was doing when he sacked Roberts, and when he had the cellar enlarged, and when he began rising early each morning. He fixed one of the lights so that it would concentrate on the target he had made—leaving the rest of the cellar in darkness. I watched him from the steps when he didn't know I was there. I knew what was in his mind. Michael used to talk to himself when alone. He was going to murder Major Oliver . . ."

"I thought so," said Knollis.

"One thing I did not know was *when*," went on Rhoda Maddison, "so I had to hurry. I had it all planned for that morning. I had been waiting for an opportunity, and when Gillian rang the previous night to say she would be staying in Maunsby—"

"Then it was you who fixed the celluloid strip in the door!" said Knollis.

"Who else?" Rhoda asked caustically. "I had to make it look as if someone had entered the inn, hadn't I? If the place was locked, and I was the only person at home with Michael . . . !"

"Yes, of course," Knollis said in a humble voice. "And then, Miss Maddison?"

"As soon as I heard Michael bumping about in the cellar I went down with my bow."

"The arrows?" interrupted Knollis. "It was you who took them from the bar?"

Rhoda Maddison smiled enigmatically. "No, but I knew who had taken them, and I knew where they were, and it *wasn't* my brother!"

"Who was it?" Knollis asked brusquely.

"That is a mystery for *you* to solve," Rhoda replied. "The mystery *I* had to solve was who had taken them from their hiding place in the golf bag. As they had gone, I suspected Michael, and decided to play a game with him. I would go down the cellar and pretend to show him how to shoot, waiting my time until I got a chance to shoot him with one of the hunting arrows. There would only have been the two of us there, so I was not afraid of witnesses!"

"And then?"

"I went down the cellar, Inspector, and found Michael lying beneath the target. All the lights were on, and the wine store door was open. There was glass on the floor, and the broken bottle stood on top of the racks. Michael was dying, and I remembered to smile at him. Then I heard someone walk over the doors of the delivery chute toward the side door, so I switched off all the lights but the target one, hid in the wine store, and shot the bolt across. I watched through a chink between the planks of the door and saw Gillian enter the cellar."

"Then it definitely wasn't Miss Gillian who killed your brother?" asked Knollis.

"That is one thing I'll swear in any court, Inspector. I was the first to find Michael, and he was then pierced by the arrow and dying. Yes, I'll swear that, and heaven knows I owe Gillian no love! The fluffy little Gillian was facing death for the first time in her life—her parents had been killed in a raid, but she never saw them. She learned a great deal in those short seconds! I could see her mind working behind that smooth forehead and those clear blue eyes. She grew up in that minute, Inspector. She also knew someone was in the wine store, and if she had opened the door—she couldn't have of course, but if she had, or if she had gone to my room—"

"She would have died like her uncle," said Knollis.

Rhoda nodded, calmly and undramatically.

"She switched off the remaining light and ran back to the ground floor. I waited, and listened, but she went out, so I went back to my room, took apart my bow, put it in its case, undressed, and got into bed."

She gave Knollis a long slow smile. "This will shock you, Inspector Knollis, but I went to sleep and really was asleep until Rose Cromwell awoke me."

"That doesn't surprise me at all," replied Knollis.

Rhoda released her fingers, and her hands sprang apart in a gesture of finality. "That's that! Have another whisky, Inspector!"

"I—yes, I can do with it," said Knollis.

"I'll have one with you," she said.

When both glasses were charged she raised her own, smiling mockingly over the rim. "Good luck!"

"Good luck," Knollis said in a more subdued voice than was normal to him.

"A nice drink, of good vintage, Inspector!"

"Yes. Yes, it is good whisky."

"You can now say you've shared a bottle with a murderer, Inspector Knollis! This was the bottle broached by my brother's slayer! He is obviously a man of good taste!"

Knollis's lips came away from the glass for a split second, and then he threw back his head and tossed the two fingers of neat whisky down his throat.

"Why a man?" he asked.

"Women seldom drink it—not in moments of stress, anyway," Rhoda replied. "They fly to the brandy bottle. Doesn't that give you a clue?"

"I need no more clues," said Knollis, snatching at his hat. "I know my man!"

"You only need *proof* now," she said.

He paused in the doorway, and half-turned. "You swear you have told me the truth, Miss Maddison?"

"I've already sworn that I've told you the truth, Inspector Knollis. I told you it was the first and last time. I told you the truth in both instances."

"Thanks," said Knollis, and left the inn.

Once outside he realised that Lancaster had taken the car to Maunsby, and would now be superintending the raking-over of the corporation ash and rubbish heaps for the broken bottle and whatever fingerprints there might be left on it.

That was an auxiliary clue, one that would support the theory he now intended to prove. There was no car, so he would walk, but first he had to get rid of Major Oliver.

After a moment's thought he went into the call-box opposite the Fox and sought the major's telephone number in the directory. Then he dialled him, and asked him if could spare the time to slip over to Maunsby to see Inspector Lancaster. There was a point, he emphasised, on which the major could advise him— and yes, perhaps there would be a few supplementary questions. They would be most grateful, and yes, immediately.

The door of the box slammed behind Knollis as he walked briskly down Uppercroft Lane, satisfied that Major Oliver would take the short cut to Maunsby via his own lane.

Outside the Wain Inn he found one of Lancaster's men, watching Woodstock House.

"Major Oliver gone out yet?" he asked.

"No, sir, but it looks as if he's going. I had a signal from Morgan—he's in the hedge-bottom at the far side of the field."

"I'd better wait with you," said Knollis.

Five minutes later he saw for himself as the major's car moved easily along the lane toward Maunsby.

"You can call your friends in and get back to town now," he said. "That was all we wanted you to do."

He met Captain Saunders at the foot of the lane, walking to the Fox, he explained, for a drop of that which cheers and to have a word with two of the Teverby Bowmen he would find there. "Never did like drinking in the house, anyway, so it gives me an excuse! Seen Miss Maddison lately? I was wondering how she's bearing up."

"Can you imagine her being other than normal?" Knollis asked with a slight trace of bitterness.

Saunders looked at him, and then laughed. "No, I can't. Being married to her would be like being married to a sphinx. She'd get what she wanted, and then eat you up."

"Making a pretty marvellous Black Widow!" said Knollis.

"By the way," said Saunders as he moved off; "we have an archery do on tomorrow afternoon. I wondered if you might care to come and watch. Might give you a few ideas, you know!"

"Not a bad notion," said Knollis. "Something special, or just a local derby?"

"County Association's shoot for the Golden Arrow. We've some star entries. Two-thirty on the field opposite my place."

"I hope to be there," said Knollis.

He trudged up the lane, easing his collar from his neck and wondering why conventional Englishmen weren't allowed to wear something more comfortable than yak-collars, at which he gave a grim laugh.

Johnson, Major Oliver's man, didn't take kindly to being questioned about his master in his master's absence, and he was sure his master wouldn't like it.

"You know what your master can do," said Knollis, who was rapidly losing his temper with the case. "I'm here to ask questions, and you are to answer them, master or no master—unless you care to run into town to the police station!" Johnson did not think he would like that.

"Now then," said Knollis. "You remember the day on which Mr. Maddison was killed?"

"Yes, sir," said Johnson.

"You're sure you remember it?"

"I'm certain, sir."

"What makes you remember it?"

"It was the day Mr. Maddison was murdered, sir!"

Knollis buried his face in his hands and prayed for patience, patience beyond the normal experience of mortal beings. "Can you remember it for any other reason?" asked Knollis.

"Well," said Johnson, a lanky individual with hair like dark brown seaweed, "that was the day the master started singing round the house."

"Doesn't he usually sing round the house?"

"Only those belly noises he does for his Yoga business—o-o-ohm, o-o-ohm—that sound like a cow in labour."

"I take it you don't go for Yoga," said Knollis.

"I don't understand it, sir," said Johnson.

"Neither do I," said Knollis, "so we won't criticise what we don't understand. Anyway, he hadn't been singing round the house?"

"Not for a good many months, sir. Then the paper-boy came and told me about poor Mr. Maddison, and I told the master, and that was when he started to sing."

"Not before?" asked Knollis with upraised brows.

"No, sir."

"Damn!" said Knollis, a rare event with him.

Johnson stood looking at him as if he was from another world.

"Any idea what time the major went to bed on the previous night?"

"He didn't sir. He never does in hot weather."

"When the deuce does he sleep?" asked Knollis.

"After dawn breaks, sir. Then he has a couple of hours and wakes as fresh as a daisy."

"Wakes himself?" asked Knollis, slowly feeling his way toward the information he sought.

"No, sir, I wake him with a cup of tea without milk or sugar."

Knollis cleared his throat. "Er—Johnson, since you can remember this day so well, perhaps you can tell me at what time you awoke him on this particular morning, the morning on which Mr. Maddison was murdered. Can you?"

Johnson nodded his head in a significant manner.

"I can that, sir! You see, sir, he'd had me up twice in the night to brew tea for him, and when it got to six o'clock I lay in bed, and thought about it, and I said to myself as the old so-and-so could overlay for once."

"I see," said Knollis, feeling a tremor in the neighbourhood of his solar plexus.

"I was all in, sir!" whined Johnson. "Couldn't get to sleep when I first went to bed—for the heat, and then he has me up twice to brew tea, and then expects me in his room—not only up, but in his room with another brew at six o'clock! I mean, sir!"

"I see your point," said Knollis. "Er—then at what time did you wake him?"

"I didn't, sir. He woke me! I woke up with a start to find him standing beside the bed with a cup of tea in his hand. *Must be All-Fool's Day*, he says. *The master waits on the servant, waking him, and cherishing him.* And then he starts to swear! Lord, can he swear. There isn't a regimental s'arnt-major in the country as can beat him—"

"The time, Johnson? The time?" Knollis asked urgently.

"Twenty-five past six by the alarm clock on the table beside my bed, sir. I keeps it on by the wireless, and it doesn't lose more than two minutes a day."

"Look," Knollis said cautiously, "you are sure it was the same day?"

"I swear it, sir, because he was so nice to me after. Said he was sorry for swearing at me, and gave me a quid for a drink. Yes, sir, it was exactly the same morning as Mr. Maddison got done in."

"Thanks, Johnson," said Knollis.

He walked down the drive, and down the lane, his head bent low as he kicked despondently at such small stones as came within range of his shoes. He walked into the Wain and asked the landlord for the use of his telephone, and firmly closed the door before he dialled police headquarters at Maunsby.

"I want Inspector Lancaster," he said.

Lancaster had to be found. He was out in the courtyard, watching the sorting of bottles and cans culled from a disused sand quarry.

"Lanky there?" Knollis said when at last his colleague came to the 'phone. "Knollis here. I'm at the Wain at Teverby, drowning my sorrows—or going to do so. Can you send a car for me? Yes, the game's up. They've all got unbreakable alibis, and we'll have a conference with the C.C., and I can only advise him to close the case. We're whacked, Lancaster, by somebody far cleverer than ourselves."

"You telling me that?" snorted Lancaster down the wires. "I'm coming out to help you drown. From a broken bottle in the dustbin! I'd like to tell Miss Rhoda Maddison what I really think of her!"

"Oh, and why?" asked Knollis.

"You know how these bottle labels are punctured with code numbers? So we can say what came from which batch?"

"Of course," said Knollis. "Get on with it, man!"

"Well, we found where the Teverby stuff was chucked out from the carts, and the men could say within a yard or two which was the Wednesday batches—were—was—I don't care which it is. The point is that there are five, no less than five Fox whisky bottles, all with their necks knocked off, and all polished as pretty as you like, so that there isn't a fingerprint between 'em. As you say, we're finished."

CHAPTER XVI
AN ASSEMBLY OF TOXOPHILITES

THE NEXT AFTERNOON was one of those cloudless, hazy-blue-skied days which an English summer can produce on occasion, truly King's weather, and Lancaster sat beneath the hawthorn trees which divided the archery field and watched Knollis sprawling on the grass on his back with his trilby cocked over his eyes, more than thoughtfully.

It was queer how controlled some men could be, and when he thought of Knollis, and then thought of the Yoga-practising Major Saunders and his alleged self-controlled emotions he had to laugh. That morning, at a conference, Knollis had gone stage by stage through the case for the benefit of the Chief Constable of the County, and the County Superintendent of the C.I.D. His face like that of a poker-player, he had displayed motives one by one, dealt with times, and places and persons as if they were no more than counters in a child's game. He had shown how

Rhoda Maddison could have committed the murder. He had shown how Major Oliver could have done it, and he had shown why neither Captain Harry Saunders nor his wife Gillian could be held responsible.

"As I see it," he said in his best lecturing voice, "Maddison could have been murdered by Rhoda Maddison, or by Major Saunders, or by the pair of them working together. On the present evidence we will never be able to prove it, and neither you, sir, nor I, dare put the dossier before the Director of Public Prosecutions and ask him to consider it. Frankly, we are beaten. I've done my best, and that best has solved seven previous cases."

He shrugged his shoulders.

"I've let my own record down, but there you are, and we can't expect to get one hundred per cent. results even if we always hope for them."

The Chief Constable leaned back in his chair and gave a deep sigh of disappointment. "I'm sorry, Inspector—and sorry for you as well as ourselves. We'll keep the case open, of course, and if new evidence should arrive we'll ask for you again, but I have to agree that you can do nothing more as the case stands. It's a pity. I hate to see a murderer get away with it."

And now Knollis was lying on his back with features as serene as a June bride.

Still, it was a glorious day. Higher up the field six large archery targets stood in a line, each four feet in diameter, and colourful with their rings of white, black, light blue, and red, and the gold centres. Saunders, as Field Captain, had been busy with measuring tapes, and had run three white strings across the field parallel with the targets, and distances of eighty, sixty, and fifty yards from them. A Hereford Round was to be shot; six dozen arrows at the longest distance, four dozen at the middle distance, and two dozen at the shortest.

Beside him, in the only shade to be found on the field, were archers from all parts of the county, unpacking their equipment and talking archery as hard as they could go. A few of the men were dressed in ordinary workaday clothes, but the majority wore white flannels and Lincoln green shirts, with long-peaked green caps, each with its club badge pinned or embroidered on it. The ladies in the main wore green skirts and variously coloured shirt-blouses. Gillian Saunders was strolling about the field particularly trim in green slacks and a golden-yellow sweater which revealed her figure admirably, a fact of which she was well aware.

"She's nice," commented Lancaster.

Knollis rolled over and propped his chin on his hands. "You mean Mrs. Saunders?"

"Who else?" muttered Lancaster. "She stands out like a peacock in a field of barn-door hens."

"A very apt simile," said Knollis.

"She's rather a nice girl," said Lancaster. "Her husband knows how to pick 'em."

"He certainly picked a right one in Gillian," said Knollis. "If it wasn't for her evidence he'd be in the cells now—whether he had murdered Maddison or not."

"Y'know," said Lancaster. "I feel pretty much as the C.C. does about this affair; I'm more sorry for you than for ourselves."

"Excuse me!"

A girl calmly stepped over Knollis and went running up the field toward Captain Saunders.

"Oh, Harry! My bow-string is going, and I simply dare not use it, and I left my spares at home. Can you fix me up, you dear?"

"He's my dear now," called Gillian from the middle of the field. "Lay off, *darling*!"

"He'll still be a dear if he can fix me up!"

"Help yourself," Saunders shouted back. "They are on the table in the archery room."

The girl ran up the field, and between the targets to the rickety five-barred gate that led on to the road. Knollis watched her go, watched her cross the road, and run between the yew hedges to the door of the archery room in the west wing of Ellwood House.

"See, Alfred Bates sleeps in the east wing, and at the back, doesn't he?" Knollis asked in a lazy voice.

"So he said," muttered Lancaster, more interested in the activities around him than in a case that was now closed.

"And all the domestic quarters are at the east end of the building!"

"Er—yes."

Knollis got to his feet and stretched himself. "I'm going to borrow the car and slip along to the Wain for a snifter. It's only half-past two, and they look like starting at least twenty minutes behind schedule."

"I'll come with you," said Lancaster.

In a low voice Knollis replied: "You please stay put, Lanky, my friend. I have a job to do—one that wouldn't appeal to you. In any case I need you here. If any of them show signs of leaving by car, don't ask any questions of anybody, but 'phone headquarters from Saunders' place and sound the general alarm."

Lancaster looked up excitedly. "You mean you've got something, Knollis? Really got something?"

Knollis looked round to make sure no one was listening, and then from the corner of his mouth said: "The brain is working now it's had a rest. See you later!"

"Not going, are you?" Saunders shouted to him as he strolled up the field to his car.

"Man about a dog!" replied Knollis.

"Oh, sorry! Yes, of course!"

Knollis paused before getting into the car, and looked at the colourful scene laid out before him. His people were all in one neat parcel, ready to be grabbed if needed. Captain Saunders was dashing about, arranging things and people. Gillian was strolling around, flaunting her figure and her auburn hair. Rhoda Maddison, newly arrived, was strapping a bracer on her left forearm, while Major Oliver, who had come with her, was sitting on a log in the hedge-bottom regarding her with an adoring expression. Lancaster was also there. All was right with the world, for the time being at least.

He drove up the hill at a gentle pace, coasted idly down the other side, slipped into gear again as he reached the Wain Inn, and so to the Fox, where he got out of the car and went into the inn, looking for Rose Cromwell.

He called for a light ale, and asked Rose if she would have a drink with him. She smirked, and accepted a pink gin.

"Is Mr. Williams, the farmer, in the house?" Knollis asked casually.

"In the smoke, sir. Shall I put your drink through?"

"Many in?"

"Only three, sir."

"Yes, please put my drink through, and fill Mr. Williams' again."

He went through and introduced himself to the farmer.

"I know you by sight, of course, Inspector," said Williams, a man like a house-side.

"I'd like to ask you a question or two," said Knollis.

The farmer's companions began to move away.

"You needn't go," said Knollis, "but I will ask you to regard all this as confidential until, say, this evening, and then it won't matter one way or the other. Now, Mr. Williams, I understand you were in this room the night when Captain Saunders brought his hunting arrows to show to Major Oliver?"

"Yes, there were just the three of us, plus Mr. Maddison."

"Now I don't want to prompt your imagination, but I'd like you to tell me as clearly as you can what happened about the arrows when the coach party invaded the inn."

The farmer scratched his head. "Well, Saunders sort of thoughtfully tested the points, and then said it might be wise for Maddison to put them behind the bar for the time being—just in case the coach party were in a skylarking mood. So Maddison took them behind the bar with him, and then called Saunders' attention to show him where they were, and to tell him he could reach them when he was ready to go."

"He actually said that?" exclaimed Knollis. "That Captain Saunders would be able to reach them when he was ready to go?"

"He said that, sir. I heard him distinctly."

"Now look," said Knollis, showing signs of excitement, "did either of the men leave this room before the arrows were missed?"

"They both did. Major Oliver wondered if he ought to put his parking lights on, because he'd left his car on the street. He said he'd dropped in for one, and then got talking and forgot all about time."

"Did he go near the serving hatch—the half-door?"

"No—o, I'll say he didn't, Inspector."

"How long after did Saunders go?"

"Two minutes or so. I didn't see what he did, because Jill Maddison was serving my table with a tray of drinks, and she was between me and the hatch."

"So that was it!" Knollis murmured to himself.

Williams poured his bottle and said: "Cheerio, sir!"

"Cheerio!" Knollis said absently. "Look, Mr. Williams, did Saunders make much of a song and dance when he missed his arrows?"

"Well, yes, he did. He nearly turned the house upside down. He blackguarded Maddison, and even swore mildly at Jill—several of us called him to order for that, and he apologised."

Knollis drained his glass to the bottom. "Mr. Williams, you're the best friend I've met in Teverby. We'll have another together later."

He almost ran from the Fox, and jumped into his car, glancing at the dashboard clock as he switched on the engine. Back at headquarters in Maunsby he called for a lady's cycle and a car driver. One of the policewomen lent her cycle, and then Knollis gave his orders to the driver.

"You're to follow me in the car. You needn't start straight away, providing you get to the Fox at Teverby at the same time as I do."

He wheeled the cycle to the street, and rode through the town to Canal Street. Here he checked his watch, and then rode as fast as he could on the low-geared cycle to the Fox, where he again checked the time and wiped the sweat from his face and neck. He propped the cycle against the wall, walked into the inn, and straight down the cellar steps. He watched two minutes tick away, and then went back to his cycle and set off down Uppercroft Lane. The car had now caught him up and was proceeding in a stately fashion behind him. He kept well in to the hedge so that he would not be seen from the archery field, and braked when within twenty yards of Ellwood House. Here he took out his watch again and let four minutes go by, then opened the boot of the car and literally crammed the bicycle into it, regardless of any damage he might be causing to either cycle or car.

"Now drive like blazes to the tow-path of Canal Street!" he ordered as he climbed in beside the driver.

At Canal Street he checked with his watch again, and made a few notes.

"Back to the Fox now," he said to the bewildered driver. "And I haven't gone mad, so don't look at me like that!"

Once more at the Fox, Knollis dragged the cycle from the boot and told the driver to return to headquarters, there to wait for him. Then he cycled over the hill to Maunsby, threaded his way through the town to Canal Street yet again, and there consulted his watch before allowing his now red and perspiring features to break into an unusually wide smile. He rode back to headquarters at a sedate pace, delivered the cycle to the policewoman with his compliments and told her to report if the cycle was damaged in any way. "You should be proud of it," he smiled. "It has solved the Maddison murder case."

In Lancaster's office he called for a pot of tea, and then had a wash. Two of Lancaster's sergeants and one of his detective-officers were hanging around the room, and Sergeant MacFarlane asked if there was anything else Knollis wanted. His manner indicated that he was quite sure that the heat had affected the Scotland Yard man.

"Anything else?" asked Knollis as he sipped his tea gratefully. "Yes, a pair of handcuffs. We might have trouble!"

Then he smiled. "I know what you're all thinking, but I'm not. Look, this is a whacking great pot of tea, so why not get more cups and all join me?"

"Er—you've—er got the case stitched up, sir?" MacFarlane asked cautiously.

"I've got it stitched up—thanks to the cycle," said Knollis. "Lord, I didn't know a lean man like myself could produce so much sweat. One of you get on that typewriter and take down a note for your chief. Ready? *Inspector Lancaster: I'm sending Bates down to tell Gillian she is wanted urgently on the phone at Ellwood House. Stay put unless Saunders follows her, in which case come after him. Knollis.* It doesn't need signing, so shove it in an envelope and seal it, and then address it to him."

After a second cup of tea Knollis rose. "I'd better take you all, and I'll drive."

"Gillian Maddison, eh?" murmured MacFarlane. "Well, this's a turn-up for the book, if you like! I don't particularly like arresting women for murder—although I admit they're more capable of it than men. More callous, and hard-hearted."

"Sergeant," Knollis said gently, "we can manage without your lecture on feminine psychology. I'm trying to think!"

The rest of the journey was made in silence. Knollis again drew up a few yards from Ellwood House, and well within the lee of the ledge.

"You'll all stay here while I go to the house," he said. "You stay put unless Captain Saunders follows his wife from the field—"

"When we turn in to deal with any rough stuff?" said Mac-Farlane.

"Correct," said Knollis.

He went to the house, asked to use the phone, and used it with the receiver rest held down. Then he laid the receiver on the table and called Bates from the hall. "Oh, Bates! I wonder if you would slip down and tell Mrs. Saunders she is wanted on the 'phone, and that it is urgent?"

"Yes, sir."

"Oh, and perhaps you wouldn't mind giving this to Inspector Lancaster while on the field?"

"Pleasure, sir."

Knollis watched Bates go, and replaced the receiver. He stood looking out at the garden for a minute, and then gave vent to an exclamation. He ran from the house to the car.

"MacFarlane! Do you know a little man called Kesteven? Makes bows and arrows, and is woodwork master at some school or other?"

"I do," said the detective-officer.

"Know where he lives?"

"Why yes, sir. He—"

"Fetch him—by the scruff of his neck if necessary. If you've never seen a short-sighted fool before you're seeing one now! Get out, MacFarlane, and let the man get on his way. Now off you go, and never mind speed limits!"

"And what do I do now?" asked MacFarlane as he stood in the roadway with Knollis.

"Disguise yourself as a sawn-off tree trunk," said Knollis, and stalked back to Ellwood House.

Gillian Saunders followed him in.

"Why, hello, Inspector! Excuse me a minute, won't you? I'm wanted on the telephone."

"Sorry to have had to lie to you," said Knollis, "but I wanted to see you privately. There was no 'phone message."

"But I'm in the middle of a shoot! I'll miss my end!"

"End?" asked Knollis.

"An end is six arrows—or three—we each shoot at the target before stepping back to let the next competitor shoot. I'll miss my ends."

"Sorry about that," said Knollis, "because I wanted to tell you about a bike-ride I've recently undertaken."

"Oh, tell me later!" Gillian snapped, and began to hurry to the door.

"You won't like me to tell you in front of your fellow-archers," said Knollis.

Gillian turned, her neat figure silhouetted in the doorway. "What—what do you mean?"

"I borrowed a lady's cycle, and cycled from Canal Street to the Fox, and then to here. I then put the cycle in the boot of a police car and was driven to Canal Street. I then came back to the Fox and biked from there to the house of Sally Denby in Canal Street—and I checked each journey against a watch."

Gillian's tongue reached out of her mouth to lick her upper lip, while she watched him cautiously.

"You know, Mrs. Saunders, you didn't come to Ellwood House after you found your uncle Michael dying in the cellar of the Fox Inn? You biked straight home to Canal Street and got into bed, in the biggest funk you've ever been in throughout your life!"

"I—I . . ." she stammered.

Then Captain Saunders appeared behind her in the doorway, with Lancaster hard on his heels.

"What the dickens are you playing at, Gillian? You've missed your end. You'll have to take your place on the line, you know!"

"Nobody will miss the end," said Knollis. "It's very close at hand. I've just been telling your wife, Captain Saunders, about a few cycle rides I've had . . ."

He once more told the story, not forgetting to mention that he had used his watch to some purpose.

"I don't get it!" said Saunders, pushing past his wife to face Knollis. "What's it all about?"

"Just this," said Knollis. "In the time stated, she couldn't have biked down here from the Fox and been taken back to Canal Street by you in the car."

"Well?"

"Your—er—end!" said Knollis. "I've shot my six!"

"You're not accusing my wife of—of murdering Maddison are you?"

"No, I can prove that she didn't murder him. The person in the wine cellar has sworn to that."

Gillian's hand went out to grasp the arm of the monk's bench on her left. "Who—who was it—in the wine store?"

"Your aunt."

"Then it was she! Oh, and I thought—I thought—! Oh, why did I ever let such a thought enter my head!"

"You thought it was your husband, didn't you?" said Knollis. "That's why I know you didn't come here when you left the inn. You just dare not come here and discover that he wasn't at home, and in bed! That's why you made up the story about cycling hell-bent to see him, and finding him here. And then, as you had started the story, your husband had to confirm it. Isn't that correct, Captain Saunders?"

Saunders gave a rueful shrug. "Obviously, yes. I knew all along that she thought I'd done the job, although she daren't admit it even to herself."

"There's another point," said Knollis.

Saunders grinned. "There always is!"

"But few supplementaries this time," said Knollis, and smiled back at him.

"You took your own hunting arrows from the shelf behind the bar at the Fox, didn't you?"

Saunders hesitated. "Er—yes! How did you find out?"

"That's my business," said Knollis, while Lancaster stood with his back to the wall and a queer expression on his face, obviously not knowing anything that was in his colleague's mind.

"Why did you take them?" asked Knollis. "Why all the mystery about the business? Can you explain?"

"Why, I mean, you see, it was like this," Saunders began lamely.

At that moment Charles Kesteven came hurriedly into the house, propelled somewhat brusquely by the sergeant. "Mr. Kesteven, sir!"

Knollis turned. "Hello, Mr. Kesteven! Sorry to snatch you from your rural quietude like this, but I need your evidence. Didn't you tell me you had lent your Mongol bow to someone, and that it was returned the day before yesterday?"

Kesteven nodded. "Yes, I lent it to Captain Saunders. He was to give a demonstration somewhere. It looked to me as if he had taken off the original string, and used a thinner one with modern arrows. There was a new ridge in the bed of each nock."

"Did you give a demonstration, Captain Saunders?" asked Knollis.

"Er—yes."

"Where? In the cellar of the Fox Inn, to Michael Maddison? On Michael Maddison?"

"Harry!" shrieked Gillian Saunders. "Tell them it is all wrong! You didn't kill Michael! You didn't! You didn't!"

Saunders turned to bolt, but Lancaster's long legs went out, and Saunders fell across the threshold, grazing his face on the iron scraper-mat. Lancaster helped him to his feet.

"Was it Saunders?" he asked incredulously.

"It couldn't have been anyone else," said Knollis. "It was all so easy for him, Lancaster. I saw it as I lay on the archery field and looked toward the house. He biked to the inn, exactly as he had suggested, with Mr. Kesteven's bow fastened to the frame of the cycle. On his return he parked the bike, entered the house by way of the archery room, and went straight to bed. By using the archery room he could get in without Bates hearing him."

Knollis paused, and then went on: "Why did he kill Maddison? I'll tell you why. He and Oliver had exchanged confidences, and Oliver had pitched the story about Maddison blackmailing him. Saunders is no fool, and realised that the boot was on the other foot. He intended marrying Gillian, but he wasn't averse to having her money as a dowry, and if Oliver continued to blackmail Maddison there wasn't going to be much left."

He smiled at Saunders. "There was, naturally, another point. If Oliver was getting Maddison's money, and Rhoda Maddison was going to marry him, then it meant that she was going to get Gillian's money, and get Michael's money—if any—on his death, and Saunders didn't see why Rhoda should have it all. He knew of the existence of Major Oliver's Mongol bows, and he knew Mr. Kesteven possessed one. The rest is as plain as a pike-staff. Kill Maddison with a short bow in a low cellar, and even people as unlearned as we are about archery matters must jump to the inevitable conclusion sooner or later. He knew of Oliver's queer habit of wandering about at all hours of the night, and that was his only real slip, because he had to rely on a fortuitous circumstance—Oliver being unable to account for his movements at twenty minutes past six on the vital morning. He was unlucky, Major Oliver had the best of alibis."

Major Oliver came breasting boisterously into the house, demanding in a loud voice to be told what was happening.

Gillian glanced at her husband, and suddenly charged past Knollis into the library, and through it to the archery room, slamming the door and locking it.

"Get her!" said Knollis.

And that was where both he and Lancaster slipped. Saunders suddenly grasped Major Oliver by his bull-like neck and thrust him against Lancaster. Lancaster reeled back, and before he could recover himself Saunders had smashed the detective-officer full in the face, knocked Kesteven down with a blow to the pit of his stomach, and was speeding down the path toward the gate. MacFarlane saw him coming, and ran to head him off, but Saunders forcibly thrust his way through the yew hedge and gained the sanctuary of the archery room, closing and barring the door.

"They can't get away!" snorted Lancaster. "It won't be a minute's job to smash down both doors."

Bates appeared beside him.

"He keeps his guns and revolvers in there, sir, and if you don't hurry he'll take her with him. You don't know the Captain! Once he takes hold he never lets go!"

MacFarlane was smashing his shoulder against the outer door as Lancaster and Knollis together tried to break down the inner one.

A shot sounded, and Lancaster reeled away with a bullet in his arm. Knollis skipped aside as a second one came screaming through the door. Then two more sounded at the far side of the archery room, and from the yell that followed it was possible to guess that MacFarlane also was wounded. Two more shots, and a choking cry and a moan.

It was Kesteven who resolved the situation. He calmly marched to the door, took a pair of pliers from his pocket, grasped the protruding key barrel, and turned it. He kicked the door open.

Gillian and Harry Saunders were lying in each other's arms in the middle of the floor. Saunders was dead, shot through the temple. Gillian was dying, her golden-yellow sweater bearing a rapidly growing crimson badge of death.

"Six—shots—to—an—an end, Inspector," she gasped as Knollis knelt beside her. "We—we had the—the advantage—the advantage of the Last End!"

THE END

9 781912 574391